Nisha carefully tore open the paper, exposing a length of beautiful aquamarine silk, about six meters long, along with a matching *choli* top and a petticoat. The fabric was undoubtedly meant to be worn as a sari. It was lovely, but Nisha couldn't help being disappointed. A silk sari was the *last* thing she imagined would remind *anyone* of *her*.

"So do you like the color?" Kali asked, and then immediately said, "I knew that you would." She smiled. "Feeling better?"

"It's beautiful," Nisha replied, not wanting to seem ungrateful. But as she hugged her sister again and thanked her, she knew that this present could never make her feel better about her problems.

Because a sari wouldn't stop her friends from fighting. Or help smooth things over with Brian. Or give her the courage to tell her parents about him.

And it definitely wouldn't get Nisha to the prom.

ONCE UPON A PROM

date

JEANINE LE NY

Point

ISBN-13: 978-0-545-03182-0
ISBN-10: 0-545-03182-6

Copyright © 2008 by Jeanine Le Ny
All rights reserved. Published by Scholastic Inc.

SCHOLASTIC, POINT, and associated logos are trademarks and/or registered trademarks of Scholastic Inc.

Text design by Steve Scott

12 11 10 9 8 7 6 5 4 3 2 1   8 9 10 11 12 13/0

Printed in the U.S.A.
First printing, April 2008

for Gencer

*And with many thanks
to Anne and Baba for the
lovely room overlooking the
Aegean Sea, from where this book
was completed.*

CHAPTER *One*

"Mom, Dad. I have something important to tell you," seventeen-year-old Nisha Khubani murmured as she studied her reflection in the full-length mirror in her room. Her large, almond-shaped brown eyes were earnest, which was good, but her tone . . . *Too serious,* she decided. *I don't want them to freak before they hear what I have to say.*

She cleared her throat and tried again. "Hey, guys! Guess what?" This time she smiled brightly into the mirror. "I've had a secret boyfriend for the past six months. Isn't that *crazy*? Oh, and FYI, we're going to the prom together."

1

Perfect . . . if I want to be grounded *for the rest of my life.*

Frustrated, Nisha raked a hand through her long dark curls as she turned away from the mirror. She'd have to be clinically insane to just blurt out the truth like that. Her conservative Indian-born parents would be so angry, they'd put her on the first flight to Mumbai to live with her grandmother.

Okay, maybe not.

But her mom and dad would *definitely* be upset — partly because they didn't believe in dating before marriage, partly because they thought they were being "modern" by setting Nisha up with a nice prom date named Raj, and partly because she'd been lying to them for what felt like a million years.

Nisha flopped face-first onto her white bedspread and stifled an exasperated moan with a cushy embroidered pillow. She squeezed her eyes closed, remembering the words her boyfriend, Brian Schroder, had uttered earlier that day: "*. . . either tell your* *parents that we're going to the prom together . . . or we're not going together."*

The memory pinched Nisha's heart. Of *course* she wanted to tell her parents about attending the prom with Brian, and she'd been dreaming about the magical night for months. The problem was, Nisha knew that as soon as her mom and dad found out about her boyfriend, they'd make her break up with him.

She'd seen it happen to her older sister, Kali, more than once, back when Kali was in high school. Now Kali was married and had moved away from Selina, Illinois — their sleepy Chicago suburb — to live in London with her husband, Dutta. They'd had an arranged marriage — a concept that Nisha had trouble wrapping her brain around. Having a nice husband was one thing, but how could a girl possibly marry someone before she knew if she truly loved him? Or vice versa?

But Nisha didn't have time to ponder the pros and cons of someone else choosing a someday future husband. Right now she had more pressing matters on her mind — like getting to the prom with Brian.

"Nisha!" her mom called from the kitchen downstairs. "Dinner is almost ready. Would you help me set the table?"

"Coming!" Nisha cried, her stomach suddenly rumbling. Hopefully she'd get inspired while eating her mom's famous cooking. She thundered down the steps to find her mom in the kitchen, pulling a tray of golden brown *samosas* from the oven and placing it on the stovetop to cool.

"Mmm. Smells delish, Mommy," Nisha said, grabbing for one, but her mother gently swatted her hand away.

"*Beta*, you will spoil you appetite," she said, using her pet name for Nisha, which roughly translated to *sweetheart* in English. "So, how are you? How was your day?" she asked.

"Fine and fine," Nisha answered automatically. She paused. *I've really got to stop lying,* she thought. Aside from her

4

problems with Brian, Nisha's two best friends, Jordan Taylor and Tara Macmillan, were in a major argument at the moment. "Actually, my friends are fighting — and it's bad. Really bad," she confessed, her heart heavy.

"Oh, no," Mrs. Khubani said, wiping her hands on a towel. "What is it about?"

Nisha leaned against the counter and sighed. "It's a long story," she replied, "but I'll give you the Cliff's Notes version. See, Tara accidentally told Jordan's boyfriend, Nate, that Jordan was seeing this other guy, Shane. Jordan thinks Tara did it on purpose because Tara's always had this small crush on Nate. *And* we saw Nate and Tara flirting in the school courtyard yesterday, but Tara said it was a total misunderstanding. Jordan didn't believe her so Tara got mad and . . . now they hate each other," she ended, her stomach twisting into a knot. "The worst part is that they're trying to get *me* to choose sides. But I can't, Mom. They're *both* my best friends."

"Those poor girls," Mrs. Khubani said, shaking her head. "I do not understand why these American parents let their daughters get involved with boys at such a tender age. Where is their sense?" she asked. "I think you should stay away from Jordan and Tara. Do not involve yourself in their mess."

"Um . . ." Nisha said. This was the point where, if Kali were there, she'd help Nisha explain to her mom that you can't just turn your back on your friends when their lives get a little complicated — especially when that complication involves boys. Kali was always up for a heated debate. Nisha, however, preferred to avoid confrontation. So she opened the cabinet and pulled out three dishes to set the table.

"Oh, we are five today, Nisha," Mrs. Khubani told her. "We'll have dinner in the dining room."

"Okay." Nisha gathered the extra place settings. "Who's coming?"

"You will see," Mrs. Khubani replied with a glint in her eyes. "It is a surprise."

Uh-oh, Nisha thought, carrying the plates into the dining room, not sure if she could handle another one of her mother's surprises. The last one had been an unwanted prom date. As she placed the dishes around the table, she heard the front door open. "Dad's home!" Nisha called to her mother.

"Not just Dad," a girl's voice said. And not just any girl — Kali!

"Oh, my God!" Nisha squealed, nearly dropping her last plate when she saw her sister standing in the foyer. She rushed to her, almost knocking her down with a hug. "What are you doing here?" She spotted Kali's husband struggling with two enormous suitcases, one of which, if Nisha knew her sister, was probably dedicated to half of Kali's designer shoe collection. "Hi, Dutta!" she called.

"Hey, Nisha," he grunted, dropping the suitcases by the front stairs.

"I couldn't miss my little sister's graduation, could I?" Kali said, smiling. "We came early so we could have a real visit. Oh, I

7

missed you so much!" She squeezed Nisha again.

"Me, too!" Nisha cried. She hadn't realized just how much until that very moment.

After dinner, Nisha stole away to her bedroom with Kali for a little girl talk. They'd e-mailed and talked on the phone, of course, but it wasn't the same. Nisha could hardly believe that it'd been almost a year since she'd seen her sister in person.

"Ohhhh. I am so stuffed!" Kali said, sprawling across Nisha's bed.

Nisha propped herself up with a pillow. "Maybe you should have, I don't know, *put down* the seventh *samosa*?" she said, teasing her.

"No way. I'm going to eat Mom's food until I burst!" Kali declared. "I may be an excellent physician, but I'm sort of culinarily challenged. No matter how much I try, my cooking just isn't edible."

"I could have told you *that*," Nisha broke

in. "I used to dump all those after-school cheese 'surprises' you made me in the trash."

"You did not!" Kali laughed and thumped Nisha with a pillow. "Well, all I have to say is thank goodness for take-out. Dutta isn't much better than me in the kitchen."

Nisha noticed how her sister's face lit up whenever she mentioned her husband. "You guys seem really happy together," she remarked. "I guess married life suits you."

"Actually? I had no idea it was going to be this good," Kali admitted. "It's so amazing when you realize you love somebody with all your heart. I guess it's a little scary, too. But now I can't imagine my life without Dutta." She reached out to sweep a few stray hairs away from Nisha's eyes. "You'll know what I'm talking about one day."

I think I already do, Nisha thought as Brian instantly came to her mind. She smiled and regarded her older sister, who was wearing an elegant green silk tunic over her wide-legged jeans — a far cry from the tight

9

Lycra minidresses she used to sneak out of the house wearing. In some ways, her sister was just like the old Kali Nisha remembered — funny and smart and always ready to laugh — but she certainly wasn't the wild and rebellious Kali Nisha had grown up with. "You're different," Nisha blurted.

"How so?" Kali asked, and Nisha shrugged.

"I don't know. I guess more mature? Centered?"

"Maybe it's because I discovered the meaning of life in England," Kali said. She quickly flipped into a cross-legged position, closed her eyes, and pretended to meditate. "Ommmmmmmmm."

Nisha laughed again and threw a pillow at her. "You dork, I'm trying to be serious!"

"I know. I'm sorry," Kali said, opening her eyes. She scooted closer to Nisha. "So. Are you going to tell me why you're so stressed?" she asked.

Nisha winced. "Is it that obvious?"

"Only because I know you better than anyone," Kali replied. "You kept drifting off into your own world at dinner. Let me guess. Something to do with your boyfriend?" Kali knew all about Brian. Nisha had even called her in desperation a few weeks ago when Brian had first mentioned that he wanted to meet their parents.

"Remember when you told me not to introduce Brian to Mom and Dad?" she began, and Kali nodded. "Well, *that* kind of blew up in my face. Mom and Dad want me to go to the prom with this Indian boy they know. Brian found out about it, and now he's mad because he thinks I'll never tell them about him."

"Isn't he right, though?" Kali asked. "I mean, if you had a choice you *wouldn't* tell them."

Nisha glanced at Kali. "Uh, way to be *helpful*, sis," she said sarcastically. "How about one of your magical schemes to get me out of this instead? I need your *advice*! What should I do?" Now that Nisha was having tension with her friends, she needed Kali more than ever.

Kali seemed to ponder the issue. After a few minutes she said, "I think the only thing you can do, Nisha, is embrace it."

"Huh?" Nisha asked, confused. "Embrace what?"

"Look, you said that I'm different now, and you're right," Kali told her. "When I was a teenager I spent all my time hanging out with my crazy friends, slipping out of the house at night to go to parties, and dating tons of boys."

"I remember," Nisha said. "It was incredible what you got away with."

"Yeah, but truthfully, I wasn't comfortable with all that. I was only pretending to be this wild girl so that I could roll with them," Kali explained. "During college and med school, when I was on my own, I figured out what I wanted in life. I *embraced* it. Then Mom and Dad introduced me to Dutta and we got married. . . . Now I feel as if I'm finally in the right place."

Nisha squinted, slightly annoyed. "Are you saying I need to have an arranged marriage to an Indian guy to be happy?" she asked, really hoping that wasn't the case.

"Not necessarily," Kali said, shaking her head. "I'm telling you to figure out who you want to be and then just . . . *be* it. You shouldn't care what anybody else thinks." She rolled off the bed and stood. "Hey, maybe I have something that'll help. Wait here, okay? I'll be right back."

As Kali exited the bedroom, Nisha considered the advice her sister had shared. *Just be it?* It sounded like an advertising slogan. Plus Nisha already had an idea of who she wanted to be. *A regular teenage girl who's carefree and in love with her boyfriend. Plain and simple,* she thought, knowing full well that her parents would never stand for it. *Just be it. How? I'm not thousands of miles away from our parents, free to do whatever I please, like Kali is . . . yet.*

Moments later, Kali returned carrying a small package wrapped in bright orange tissue, tied with shiny gold ribbon. "Presents always make things better, don't they?"

Nisha's eyes widened at the sight of the gift. "Totally!" she exclaimed. "Can I open it?"

"Go for it." Kali handed over the package. "I picked this up in a shop on High Street in London. As soon as I saw it I thought of you."

"Really?" Nisha hoped it was an adorable cardigan or chunky gold bangle from that cute London store, Topshop, she'd seen on TV. She carefully tore open the paper, exposing a length of beautiful aquamarine silk, about six meters long, along with a matching *choli* top and a petticoat.

Is this supposed to be a hint? she wondered. The fabric was undoubtedly meant to be worn as a sari. It was lovely, but Nisha couldn't help being disappointed. A silk sari was the *last* thing she imagined would remind *any*one of *her*.

How about a pair of high-heeled ankle boots or a pink polka-dot bikini? Hey, even a plastic Hello Kitty purse would work. But *a sari*? Nisha didn't even know how to put one on by herself.

"So do you like the color?" Kali asked, then immediately said, "I knew that you would." She smiled. "Feeling better?"

"It's so pretty," Nisha replied, not wanting to seem ungrateful. As she hugged her sister again and thanked her for the thoughtful gift, however, she knew that this present could never make her feel better about her problems.

Because a sari wouldn't stop her friends from fighting. Or help smooth things over with Brian. Or give her the courage to tell her parents about him.

And it definitely wouldn't get Nisha to the prom.

CHAPTER *Two*

Top Ten Things a BFF Should Totally Tell You Before (or During) Prom

1) If your prom dress is a Do or a Dud
2) If your date exhibits excessively dorky behavior
3) If you sprout a sudden case of "backne"
4) If your dance moves resemble a rabid animal's
5) If your ex-boyfriend is flirting with her
6) If you have toilet paper stuck to your 4-inch rhinestone sandals
7) If you have an offensive bodily odor
8) If your stylist went psycho with the scissors and you need a wig
9) If you have spinach caught between your teeth
10) If she'll get over the stupid argument you're having with her

16

Tara Macmillan stifled a yawn, hoping her concealer was still working its magic on the dark circles beneath her chestnut-colored eyes. She was passing out "Queen Tara" buttons to her fellow Emerson High School classmates. Outside the auditorium before homeroom, she smiled and *encouraged* everyone to "Vote Tara" for prom queen but she feared that her lack of pep was showing through.

She'd spent the last two nights not even coming *close* to the eight hours of recommended shut-eye. At least the insomnia wasn't a total waste. Instead of aimlessly counting sheep Tara spent the wee hours of the morning creating her online prom presence by: 1) updating her MySpace and Facebook accounts to include her campaign agenda, 2) adding links to a newly created website dedicated solely to promoting Tara's prom queen-iness to the world, and 3) recording a video blog, stating what prom queen meant to her and posting it to the Student Shout Out page of the school's website.

But the real reason for Tara's sleeplessness was that she was feeling horribly guilty for calling her best friend, Jordan Taylor, a two-faced witch.

Tara knew she'd said it only in anger. How could Jordan believe that Tara would come on to Nate, Jordan's ex? Okay, maybe Tara had had a *slight* crush on the boy — and maybe she'd been a *tiny* bit jealous of her friend's relationship with him — but the truth was that last Monday Jordan caught Tara trying to *mend* Nate and Jordan's relationship.

It wasn't *Tara's* fault if Nate had given her an appreciative peck on the cheek right after he'd said that he wanted nothing to do with Jordan.

But all that still didn't erase the fact that Tara had to talk to Jordan at some point. *We can't let this go on much longer . . . can we?* she wondered as a familiar pain stabbed her temple — the one that invaded her head every time she thought about the fight. *Push through it, Tara.* She commanded herself to perk up and flipped her chocolate-colored hair over her shoulders.

"Don't forget to vote for Tara Macmillan for prom queen!" she called, giving away a few more buttons of her smiling face. She noticed a senior from the cheerleading squad, Ally, holding out her hand for one, which was a major surprise. Jordan was the cheerleaders' captain. Wasn't Ally supposed to be supporting her teammate? "You really want one of these?" Tara asked.

"Totally." Ally nodded. "I am *so* not voting for Jordan after what she did to Nate. So I guess it's all you."

"Um, thanks?" Tara replied, handing her a button. It wasn't exactly a vote of confidence, but she'd take it.

"Whatev." Ally's gaze shifted beyond Tara and she gasped. "Oh, my God. He's coming over here," she said in a panicky whisper. She began frantically pawing through her enormous leather tote. "Please, God, *please* let me find my lip gloss. I think he might ask me to the prom!"

"Who?" Tara held back a laugh. It wasn't long ago when *she'd* been just as anxious as Ally about finding a date for the big event. The school's mascot, Victor Kaminski, hadn't been the ideal candidate at first but Tara had accepted his invitation anyway — on the condition that she give him a make-over. After a wardrobe do-over, a cool haircut, and a little eyebrow wax, she was pleasantly surprised to find that Victor not only had an awesome personality, he was really cute, too! They'd become great friends along the way. *Maybe a little more?* Tara hoped so, but she wasn't sure.

Ally never answered Tara, but her crush was revealed when Nate Lombardo strolled by with his backpack casually slung on one shoulder and a baseball cap hiding his sandy-colored hair. "Hey, what's up, T?" he said.

"Just chillin'," Ally answered, smiling wide, her cherry-colored lips now perfectly glossed.

Nate nodded at Ally. "Cool." He turned back to Tara. "How's the campaign going?"

Tara shrugged. "Well —"

"*I'm* voting for her, that's for sure," Ally broke in. "And I bet most of the other seniors on the squad are, too."

"Nice," Nate said, then hesitated before adding, "You know, I kind of have to talk to Tara about something. In private. You don't mind, Ally, do you?"

Ally's smile faded. "Oh. No. Go right ahead. You guys have your little talk." She shot Tara an icy glare before pivoting and heading down the hall.

Tara gave a mock shiver. "Something tells me Ally's minutes away from drawing a mustache on that 'Queen Tara' pin I gave her. She likes you, you know."

Nate grabbed a pin from the box at Tara's feet. "Ally's a nice girl," he remarked, "but she needs to ease up the lip gloss. I'm more into the natural look."

"Like Jordan," Tara said, knowingly, forgetting for a second that they'd broken up. Why couldn't she keep her big mouth shut?

"Or you," Nate added. His brown eyes sparkled mischievously.

Clearly the boy had no clue how much product was in Tara's hair at the moment. But still, she could feel a hot blush creep onto her cheeks as she let out an awkward chuckle. *No way. Is Nate flirting with me?*

"So where's Victor?" Nate asked. "Didn't you say he was helping you with the prom queen thing?"

Tara scanned the hall of wall-to-wall students. "He's supposed to be here handing out promo materials with me, but I guess he blew it off," she said, disappointed.

"Oh." Nate tossed the "Queen Tara" pin between his hands. He seemed to want to say something else. "Did you . . . talk to Jordan yet?"

"No," Tara responded with a sigh. "And I have no clue when it's going to happen. We both said some pretty mean things to each other." Her head began to throb again, this time accompanied by a lump in her throat. She tried to swallow it away but couldn't.

"Oh, man." Nate's face softened when he noticed how upset Tara was. He placed an arm around her shoulders. "I'm sorry. I feel like this is my fault," he said. "I tried to explain things to Jordan yesterday but she started arguing with me. It's weird. I mean, *she's* the one who traded *me* in for a new boyfriend without telling me. If anything, *I* should be the one who's angry. Not her."

Tara nodded. Nate did have a right to be angry, but even though he was indirectly involved in the Tara-and-Jordan drama, their fight wasn't exactly his problem. "Don't worry about it," she told him. "This is between me and Jordan. It's not your fault." She looked around, observing that the crowd of students was beginning to thin. "Maybe we should get to homeroom."

"Yeah," Nate said, backing away. "See you in the lunchroom?" He was usually parked at the jock table, while Tara sat with Nisha . . . and Jordan.

"I'll be there," Tara replied as Nate strode away, though she wasn't sure whom she'd be eating with today. She bent down to gather her leather satchel and the box that held her overload of "Queen Tara" buttons and noticed a pair of blue suede Vans approaching. She gazed up, knowing exactly to whom they belonged. "Hey, if it isn't my prom-date-slash-campaign-manager extraordinaire," she said, rising up to greet him. "You missed the entire morning PR session, Victor. What happened?"

Victor stood there, motionless, holding a box of hot pink handouts for Tara's campaign. "You know what happened," he said coldly. "I don't have to spell it out for you." He held out the box for her to take. "Here. I'm done with your campaign."

"What? Why?" she asked, her heart pounding. Tara glanced at the box but wouldn't accept it. She looked at her friend, confused. "Please, Victor, you can't just quit without telling me what I did."

"Fine." Victor's hazel eyes narrowed. "Jordan told me how you and Nate Lombardo were all over each other in the courtyard the other day," he replied. "Do you really think you can just pretend to like me so I'll help you with your prom queen campaign?"

"But it's not true, Victor," she responded quickly. "And I *do* like you." She liked him more than he knew. A flash of anger surged deep inside Tara as she grasped what Jordan had done. *Jordan knew that I was starting to like Victor as more than a friend, and she exaggerated the story so that Victor would feel used and leave me dateless.*

Tara had no idea that Jordan could be so cruel. She'd acted simply to hurt Tara, and Victor was an innocent bystander. Maybe Tara had hurt Jordan, too, but she never *lied*.

Of all the sneaky, conniving, horrible . . . I can't believe I even considered *being the bigger person and apologizing first!*

"So why would your best friend say something like that if it *weren't* true?" Victor asked, arms folded over his chest, waiting for an explanation.

"Because we're not friends anymore," Tara replied, wondering now if they ever really were. "Jordan's mad about the way things turned out with Nate, and now she's blaming it all on me. She knew I'd be upset if you and I weren't friends anymore. That's why she told you that stuff."

Victor rolled his eyes. "Yeah, right."

Tara touched his arm and stared intensely into his eyes. "I'm serious, Victor. You're, like, the best guy friend I've ever had. You're nice and funny and really cute. And you've been so great about helping me with all this prom stuff. I just wish I would have realized how cool you were *before* prom season," she went on, rambling, even as her cheeks flushed. "Victor, you have to believe me on this. Jordan is a big, fat *liar*. And I don't know if I can ever forgive her for what she's done."

Tara pulled back, a bit self-conscious when she noticed Victor regarding her with his jaw dropped. *Great. Now he thinks I'm psycho.*

His expression turned from surprise to amusement. "So. You think I'm cute, huh?"

Did I really tell him how cute I think he is? "Um, a little," Tara replied, feeling her face turn even pinker. She smiled weakly. "Does this mean we're good?"

Victor nodded. "I guess I should have given you a chance to explain how *fine* you think I am before I went off on you," he said with a grin.

"Shut up!" Tara smacked him playfully on the chest.

"Okay, okay!" Victor laughed and held up his hands. "But let's do something on Friday. My treat. To make up for me being so harsh."

A date? Tara's stomach fluttered with excitement. "Sure!"

"Cool. Okay, um. Well, see you later," Victor said just as the bell rang.

Tara smiled to herself as she collected her things and headed down the hall. A pre-prom date with Victor? She was mentally flipping through all the different wardrobe possibilities when she noticed a certain blond-haired pathological liar heading in the opposite direction.

Tara's jaw clenched at the sight of Jordan. The hurt of that awful lie washed over her again.

"Hey," Tara called to a boy straggling his way to homeroom and handed him a "Queen Tara" pin. "Don't forget to vote for me," she said loud enough for the backstabber to hear. "You don't want some *two-faced witch* who cheats on her boyfriend as prom queen, do you?"

"Uh, no?" The boy took the pin.

"I didn't think so," Tara replied.

If Jordan could play cruel, then so could she.

CHAPTER *Three*

Holding a stack of lime-colored prom queen flyers to her chest, Jordan Taylor leaned against the drink machine and watched the students file into the lunchroom. *I suppose I should hand these out*, she thought, but truthfully, she was in no mood.

Probably because she couldn't stop thinking about the biting comment Tara had directed toward her before homeroom that morning. Sitting next to Tara in their assigned seats in A.P. English had certainly been no joy either. The only words Tara'd said to Jordan were, "Move your elbow."

Obviously Tara knows that I talked to Victor. It wasn't as if Jordan thought it was the *right* thing to do; she'd felt awful the moment the words escaped from her mouth. *But why can't Tara see my side of things, too?* she wondered. *Why can't she admit that she totally betrayed me?*

Yes, Jordan had started seeing Shane Dresden while she was still going out with Nate. But shouldn't she have been allowed to deal with Nate on her own terms? Instead, Tara "accidentally" told him about Shane. *Then* Jordan caught her flirting with Nate mere days after he and Jordan had broken up! So Jordan began to wonder if Tara had planned this all along. Which was why she marched right over to Victor and "accidentally" told him that she saw Tara and Nate kissing. Which was true. Sort of.

Now everything was a mess. It was less than two weeks to the prom and there were bad feelings all around, with Nisha caught in the middle. Jordan desperately wished things could go back to the way they were before all the drama — when she and her friends spent most days laughing and chatting excitedly about prom dates and dresses and dreams for what was supposed to be the most amazing night of their lives.

Yeah, right. A total fantasy.

"Vote for Jordan," she said, halfheartedly holding out leaflets for her classmates to take. She caught her breath when she spotted Tara nearing the cafeteria. She wanted to pretend that she hadn't seen her, but immediately felt the sting of Tara's cold stare. In response, Jordan lifted her chin and stood tall, hoping that she looked a hundred times more defiant than she was feeling. When Tara disappeared into the lunchroom, Jordan slumped her shoulders. *Is the day over yet?*

"Hey!" Nisha said, coming up to Jordan a few minutes later, seemingly in a great mood. "How's it going?"

"Pretty good." Jordan mustered a smile. She *wanted* to complain about how her day was totally sucking, basically due to Tara, but Jordan knew that Nisha was trying her hardest not to get dragged into the middle of their argument. "Did the Brian-talk go okay with your parents yesterday?" she asked.

"Actually, it didn't go at all," Nisha admitted. "But I *did* have a talk with my sister. She's in from England!"

"Really? That's awesome!" Jordan cried. She knew how much Nisha had missed Kali.

"I know." Nisha grinned wide, then glanced over her shoulder before saying, "So, get this. I came up with a brilliant idea last night. Instead of telling my parents about Brian, I asked Kali if she and Dutta would go on a double date with us. This way Brian will see that I told my *sister* about him. Maybe he won't care as much about meeting my mom and dad."

"Are you sure that's a good idea?" Jordan asked her.

Nisha nodded. "It's the only way, Jord.

You know how my parents are. I mean, I *want* to tell them about my boyfriend, but I'm afraid if I do they won't let me go to the prom at all."

The prom. Jordan didn't want to imagine the uncomfortable seating arrangements. The thick tension in the air mingling with the sickly-sweet scent of corsages. And forget about maneuvering around Nate on the dance floor. "Well, good luck with that," she told Nisha, hoping it all worked out for her.

"Thanks." Nisha glanced at the stack of flyers Jordan was holding. "You want to give me some of those? I'll pass them out in class." Jordan handed her a bunch and Nisha slipped them into her backpack. "You know . . ." she went on, "Tara did this whole online promotion thingy. You might want to take a look at her new prom queen website."

"She's got a *website*?" Jordan exclaimed. "Isn't that taking things a little far?"

Nisha shrugged. "You know Tara goes all out when she wants something — and she wants to win prom queen."

She probably will, if I don't get my act together, Jordan thought. *Whatever.* Who had the time for a website with classes and cheerleading and Shane? And she still had to edit down the pictures for her photography project. It was a chance to improve the D she'd gotten on her first try at an introspective series, which her teacher had deemed "fluff."

"Let's get some lunch," Jordan suggested. She and Nisha weaved around a group of chatting juniors. Before entering, Jordan peeked inside the cafeteria. Tara was at their regular table, of course, but . . . Nate was sitting next to her.

She froze, feeling a pang in her chest at the sight of the two of them, deep in conversation. *Are they talking about me? Where to go on their first date? How to reduce their carbon footprints? What?*

"You coming?" Nisha asked.

"Ummm . . ." Jordan couldn't casually arrive at the table and act as if everything were normal. She couldn't just *sit there* and watch them make eyes at each other as if it were no big deal. It was a big deal. And weird. And *ridiculous* for Nate and Tara to *think* that she'd be even *remotely* okay with it. Especially Tara.

What happened to consideration? To boundaries? To that special BFF brand of loyalty that clearly states ex-boyfriends are totally off limits *no matter how cute they are?* Jordan silently demanded. *Tara's dying to be prom queen. Soon she'll be dating Emerson High's prom king. Well, good. I hope they're happy together. . . .*

"You know, I just remembered. I have to do something," Jordan said, trying to ignore the pain in her heart. She really did have something to do. It had been on her mind for quite a while but she'd only just now decided to take action.

"What is it?" Nisha asked.

"I have to talk to Principal Harris," Jordan replied. "See you later, okay?" She bolted away from the cafeteria, up the stairs, past the Student Newz bulletin board that was decorated in the prom's "Once Upon a Time" theme, and into the principal's office.

Two days ago, Jordan had told Tara that she'd never let her have the prom queen title. But now that the dust had settled, Jordan realized that she didn't care in the least if Tara won.

For whatever reason, it seemed as though the entire student population of Emerson High had assumed that just because Jordan was popular and pretty and dating the school's star athlete, she'd want to be prom queen — without asking *her*. But now that Jordan wasn't dating the soon-to-be prom king anymore, and there was another viable candidate who actually *wanted* the title, she felt absolutely zero pressure to go through with it.

So when the school's secretary led her into Mr. Harris's office, and he looked up from his paperwork, Jordan, before she could lose her nerve, announced that she was withdrawing her name as a candidate. Then she promptly dumped her prom queen flyers into his recycling bin.

Let Tara have prom queen, she thought. *Let her have Nate, too. She can have it all.*

"Mr. Harris said it's too late to take my name off the ballot, so I'm going to just stop campaigning," Jordan told Shane Dresden the next afternoon at Joes, a funky little teahouse in downtown Selina. "I'm glad I told him, though."

Shane nodded and rested his arm along the vintage couch where they were hanging out and drinking apricot chai. "Just as long as you're definitely sure you don't want to be prom queen anymore," he said.

"I'm sure." Jordan snuggled closer, thinking it was cool of him to say that. She knew that Shane and his friends thought prom was a waste of time. Still, he'd offered to take Jordan to hers.

Shane was like no other boy Jordan had dated. For one thing he preferred dyeing his choppy uneven haircut black to match his nail polish rather than playing intramural sports. For another, he preferred listening to Peter Bjorn and John to cranking the latest Usher album. Finally, he was poetic and intense and had dreamy dark eyes that made her shiver. Jordan felt as though she could talk to Shane about anything, from the important to the mundane. Like now.

"I just felt weird about the whole thing," Jordan told him. "Prom queen was never a big deal and now, with the tension between me and Tara, I don't have the heart for a big competition. Besides, Tara's more driven and she'd probably win anyway," she added. "Did I mention that she has a website dedicated solely to Prom?"

Shane laughed, a fringe of hair falling over his right eye. "That's hardcore."

"Seriously," Jordan said. "You do *not* want to mess with this girl."

Shane laughed again. "So, should we look for my tuxedo?" he asked. "I was thinking of buying a funky retro one — the more ridiculous the better. If I have to wear a tux to the prom, I need to do it with irony."

"Well . . . maybe you *don't* have to wear one," Jordan said slowly. "Maybe we . . . won't go?" The words had left her mouth before she could stop them. Aside from the awful friction with Tara, half the Emerson cheerleaders wanted Jordan to turn in her pom-poms for breaking Nate's heart. She knew Nisha was getting fed up with choosing between her and Tara. To be pefectly honest with herself, Jordan had been considering skipping the event entirely and finally concluded that it might be best for all if she did. She wasn't going to her senior prom.

Shane eyed her carefully. "What about Nisha and her boyfriend?" he asked. "Don't you want to hang out with them at the prom?"

"Of course I do," Jordan said. "But it'll be so stressful at the table with Tara; it's bound to ruin everyone's night. And we'd have to deal with Nate. Plus, I'm sure Nisha and Brian will be too swept up in each other to do much mingling." Jordan nodded, certain in her choice.

Shane removed his mug from an old wooden end table and took a sip from it. "All right," he said. "We can do something else that night, if you want."

"Good." Jordan paused before continuing. "Shane? There's one more thing I have to do about Prom," she told him. "Right now. To make it official. Will you come with me?"

Shane took a last sip of his tea. His eyes were questioning. "Let's go," he said and followed Jordan out of Joes.

Jordan's SUV was parked by the curb across the street from the teahouse. As they approached, Jordan drew her keys from her purse and popped the trunk. She removed a long white garment bag from the car.

"What's that?" Shane asked, furrowing his brow.

"My prom dress," Jordan told him, carefully lifting up the bag to reveal the beautiful one-shouldered white silk gown. She gently swept her hand across the exquisite fabric, then said, "I'm selling it."

Jordan allowed the words to seep into her skin. If she was resolved to skip the prom, then she had to make it real. She wanted to burst into tears, but at the same time she knew she was making the right decision. She slammed the trunk closed.

Clutching the garment bag and leading the way down Main Street, Jordan recalled the wonderful day she'd found her special gown. Yes, she'd bought a pretty dress, but she'd done it with her friends. Back then, on that day, they were still having fun, laughing and sharing stories, looking forward to the prom. Together.

It was an added bonus that Jordan's gown had fit her perfectly without a single alteration and that, when she had it on, it'd seemed to make her sparkle.

Now Jordan couldn't stand to look at it.

Finally they reached Timely Treasures, a vintage consignment shop, and Jordan took a deep breath before pulling the door open. Upon entering, she spoke to an older woman with a stiff blond beehive, who seemed surprised that Jordan would want to sell such a fabulous gown with the tags still on it. "Are you sure you want to give it up?" she asked.

Jordan hesitated at first, knowing there'd be no turning back if she agreed. *It's for Prom. And you're not going, remember?*

Right, she thought. *Make it real.*

Jordan nodded. "Yes. I'm sure," she said and handed over her perfect prom gown for some other lucky girl to own.

CHAPTER *Four*

"I'll get it!" Nisha called. Her forties-
inspired, black satin minidress swished as
she raced down the stairs. Unfortunately,
her new patent leather platform heels with
the supercute ankle strap put her at a slight
disadvantage speedwise, and her mother
arrived at the door first.

"Come on in, Raj," Mrs. Khubani said.
She welcomed inside the boy whom she
thought would be Nisha's prom date.

"Good evening, Mrs. Khubani," Raj
Dixit said with his sort-of British accent. He
emerged into the foyer, looking as Euro-chic
as ever. Tonight his dark curls were slicked

back. He was wearing distressed denim, a pink button-down, a casual blazer, and unusually long and pointy shoes that seemed as though they might be painful.

Not exactly Nisha's type, but at least he was dressed as if they were about to go on a real date. Which was the important thing. The plan was to pretend that Nisha was going out with Raj and then to make the switch to Brian — without the parents *or* Brian knowing about it.

"You look very handsome, Raj," Nisha's mother commented. "Doesn't he look handsome, Nisha? Can I get you something to drink? Are you hungry, Raj?"

"Well, I —"

"Mom, we're going to dinner, remember?" Nisha cut in before Raj could answer. They were supposed to be at Brian's house in fifteen minutes and she didn't want to be late. "Kali, Dutta! Are you guys ready to go?"

Her sister and brother-in-law entered the foyer together. Kali seemed to be chewing something and Nisha gave her a questioning look. "*Samosa*," Kali replied, swallowing a mouthful of peas and potatoes.

Nisha rolled her eyes and introduced her sister and Dutta to Raj. "See you later, Mommy," she said and kissed her on the cheek. "We won't be too late."

"I still don't see why you have to take two cars," Mrs. Khubani remarked.

Nisha tensed as she tried to come up with a good-enough excuse. "Um, I thought it was a good idea, you know, in case Kali and Dutta get tired and want to go home early," she said. Thankfully her mother seemed to buy it.

Once outside Kali stretched her arms and let out an exaggerated yawn. "Gee, I'm exhausted. Dutta, maybe we should go home."

"Shh. Kali, Mom's still watching." Looking over her shoulder, Nisha glimpsed her mother peeking out from behind the living room curtains.

"You could have let me eat one of your

mum's delicious *samosas*," Raj whispered. "I'm famished."

Dutta glanced at Kali, then pulled a lumpy napkin from the pocket of his jacket. "Here, man. Last one."

Raj happily accepted it. Then he and Nisha climbed into his parents' Saab while Dutta and Kali borrowed Mrs. Khubani's Honda. Nisha began to relax when they steered away from the curb and drove to the nearby Wegmans shopping plaza. *So far so good.*

"So I think that went smoothly," Raj said when he'd parked the car.

"It was awesome, Raj. Thanks. You're my fake date in shining armor." Nisha exited the car. "Tell Pallavi I said hi, okay?" she called before getting into the Honda with Dutta and Kali. Pallavi was Raj's girlfriend, whom he'd met while attending college in Paris. Ironically, Raj's parents had no clue about his girlfriend, either, and he and Nisha had both promised to keep their secrets from all the parents.

"Well, *that* was easy," Kali commented as Raj waved and pulled away. "Beautifully orchestrated, perfectly executed, an excellent dry run for the prom. . . . If I were still sneaking out of the house to go on secret rendezvous, I'd give it a ten."

Nisha glanced cautiously at Dutta.

"Oh, he knows about everything," Kali said. "And he still loves me. Right, babe?"

"Yup. You're my firecracker." Dutta kissed her, then stepped on the gas.

"Aw, you guys make an adorable arranged couple," Nisha teased. She felt a tiny thrill when they turned down Brian's street a few minutes later. *Is this really happening? Is Brian finally about to meet my sister? I hope she likes him. I hope he likes her.*

As soon as the car stopped, Nisha burst out and ran up the path to Brian's house.

Brian opened the door before she had a chance to knock. His blond hair was slightly spiked on top and his cheeks were flushed. He seemed nervous as he gestured to his outfit. "This okay?" he asked, his blue eyes concerned.

How cute is that? Nisha thought. "You look great," she said, checking out his jeans and the crisp white shirt he had on. Instead of his usual sneakers, he wore a pair of brown loafers that seemed on the new side. "Don't worry. It's only Kali. She's pretty easygoing," Nisha assured him.

Brian took Nisha's hand in his. "Okay. Let's do this," he said.

Kali and Dutta both welcomed Brian with warm smiles as he and Nisha climbed into the backseat of the car. She held his hand as the group made friendly chitchat all the way to the Mexican restaurant and, by the time they arrived, Nisha could tell that Brian was at ease.

Once seated, they talked about everything from why Brian wanted to be an architect to Kali's heavy workload as an intern at a London hospital. Dutta mentioned his plan to start his own computer-consulting business, and Nisha talked about her dream of one day becoming a fashion editor, or designer, or both.

Toward the end of the meal, Nisha pulled Kali away from the table and into the ladies' room to find out what she thought of Brian.

"I don't like him," Kali said, her face grave, which caused Nisha to have a minor panic attack.

"What? Why not?" Nisha asked.

"Because I *love* him!" Kali squealed.

"Ohhh." Nisha rested a hand over her heart, relieved. "You scared me!"

"Nisha, he's great. He's so nice and sweet and smart," Kali went on. "Too bad —" She stopped herself.

"What?" Nisha asked even though she already knew the answer. "Too bad he's not Indian? Because Mom and Dad are going to hate him when they meet him?" Nisha finished for her sister. "That's why I'm doing *this*, Kali. So Brian and I can have one last romantic date at the prom — before Mom and Dad break us apart."

Kali nodded. "I know," she said. "And now I can see why. He really likes you. Actually, I think he *more* than likes you."

"I think I more than like him, too," Nisha admitted to her sister, blushing, and Kali gave her an understanding hug.

Back at the table, it appeared as if Nisha's plan was working. Brian seemed satisfied with meeting Kali and Dutta, and he didn't once mention being introduced to Nisha's parents — until the end of the date.

"It was really great meeting you," Brian said as Dutta stopped the car in front of Brian's house. "I hope I have this much fun when I meet your parents, Nisha." He turned to her sister. "What do you think, Kali? Will they like me?"

Nisha swallowed hard, hoping her sister would say the right thing.

"Oh, yeah. For sure," Kali replied. "But they almost know you already since Nisha talks about you nonstop."

Yes! I could kiss you, Kali, Nisha thought. It was the perfect answer.

Kali and Dutta said their good-byes, and Nisha got out of the car with Brian and walked him to the door so that she could say hers in private.

"So you talk about me nonstop, huh?" Brian grinned so wide it took over the entire lower region of his face.

Nisha shrugged. "Maybe," she said, smiling at the fact that he was smiling so much.

Then Brian leaned in to kiss her, and Nisha closed her eyes, drinking in the familiar feel of his lips.

"I can't wait for the prom," he said when they parted, and Nisha knew that he no longer needed to meet her parents before the big night.

Because he thought she talked about him all the time. But she didn't. She had never mentioned him once.

Feeling a pang of guilt, Nisha glanced away from Brian's tender gaze. "I should probably go," she said, gesturing toward Kali and Dutta, who were pretending not to stare at them from the car.

It's only until after Prom, she reminded herself. *Then I'll tell my parents about him for real.*

CHAPTER

First Dates in History

1) *Martha & George: Picnicking underneath that infamous cherry tree*
2) *Josie & Napoleon: Baking yummy flaky pastries in the kitchen*
3) *Cleopatra & Antony: Walking like Egyptians*
4) *Tara & Victor: ???*

Tara knelt on the fake grass and squinted as she pointed her miniature-golf club at the hole in question. It was a good thing she'd decided go with the simple, yet alluring, jeans-and-black-tank option for her date with Victor, as opposed to wearing the white denim micromini she'd had on first. A *mighty* good thing.

"Um, Tara?" Victor asked her. "What are you doing?"

Tara glanced up from her club. "Just aligning my shot," she told him. "What does it look like?"

"It looks like you're taking this game waaaaaay too seriously," Victor said, and then started laughing.

"But the last shot is always the hardest," Tara explained. "Not only do you have to get the angle, you have to time it so that the ball goes past the windmill blades, up the ramp, and into the hole for the free game. Don't you want to win the free game?"

Victor grinned as if she'd said the most adorable thing ever, and Tara suddenly found herself blushing.

"What?"

"Nothing," Victor replied. "You're just cute when you get all passionate about something — even if it is only miniature golf."

Tara felt her face grow even hotter, not sure if she was embarrassed about being called out on her obsessive desire to win stuff, or if it was because Victor had used the words *cute* and *passionate* in a sentence referring to *her*.

Victor surprised Tara by stepping closer and helping her to her feet. Her pulse quickened at his touch, and she could almost see the millions of tiny lightning bolts zinging from Victor's hand and tingling her arm.

Oh, my God, she thought, face-to-face with him. *I want Victor to kiss me!* She'd felt this way once before, during the prom-wear fashion show last week, but had dismissed it as a fluke.

It wasn't.

"Go for it, T-Bone," Victor said, using the nickname that Tara had always hated, but was now growing on her.

"Huh?" Was he daring her to plant one on him, right there, in the middle of Putt-Putt Paradise?

"Let's see you make a hole in one," he told her. "Show me how it's done."

"Oh." Duh. Of course he wasn't daring her to kiss him. "Okay," Tara said, trying to collect herself. *I wonder if he'll kiss me at the end of our date,* she thought, readying for the shot. *I hope so.* She swung back her club and —

"Ooh. If it isn't the happy couple."

Tara cringed as Jenny Brigger's annoying voice pierced her ears. Jenny, along with Tara, was on the prom committee, and Tara swore it was the girl's personal mission in life to give her grief. Tonight was no exception.

"Hello, Jenny." Tara turned to see her nemesis holding a golf club in one hand and shy Stuart Fullman's palm in the other. Stuart was also on the prom committee. *They're dating now?*

"What's up, guys?" Victor said.

"Funny you should ask," Jenny said. "Stuart and I scored a major coup for the prom this afternoon."

"What coup?" Tara asked. "Everything's all set."

"Well, we found this piece that's sooo amazing," Jenny cooed as Stuart nodded. "It ties in with our theme perfectly, so I went ahead and ordered it."

Tara bit her bottom lip, worried. When it came to decorations Jenny had a habit of taking the theme "Once Upon a Time" *way* too literally. It had taken Tara almost all semester to get Jenny to stop pushing for an enormous replica of the Disney castle. Not only was it expensive, but where were they supposed to put it? On the dance floor?

"What is it? You didn't score a castle, did you?" Tara asked warily.

"No. Forget that," Jenny said with a wave of a hand. "But we're not telling you what it is. Stuart and I want to keep this masterpiece a surprise," she added. "But I will say this. It's *waaaay* better than a castle. Right, Stuart?"

Stuart nodded again.

Tara felt a knot growing in the pit of her stomach.

"So, I heard through the grapevine that you still haven't bought a prom dress," Jenny continued with a smirk. "Don't you think you should get on that, O Mighty Prom Chair?"

Tara bristled. Talk about sore subjects. She'd been shopping for a dress for *weeks* — and nothing. Then, at the prom-wear fashion show, Tara had found her dream dress — a beautiful, full-skirted, purple halter number with delicate beading hand-sewn into the tulle — only to have it *stolen* away from her when Jenny won a raffle and chose Tara's dress as the prize. "Maybe you should mind your own business, Jenny."

Jenny rolled her eyes. "Look, all I'm saying is now that Jordan doesn't want to be prom queen anymore you need to look good." Tara barely had time to process this new information when Jenny added another tidbit. "I mean, can you *believe* she dropped out at the last minute? Who does Jordan think she is?" Jenny scoffed. "Oh, I know. A *loser*."

"Who are *you* to call Jordan a loser?" Tara blurted. Jordan had never said one negative thing about Jenny, although she'd had plenty of opportunities. "You know, if you're *dying* to call someone a loser, why don't you say it to your mirror?" She'd about reached her Jenny tolerance level and turned to Victor. "Let's get out of here, okay?"

And they did — but not before Tara swung her club, plunking her golf ball through the windmill, which ricocheted off the right side of the green then up the ramp and into the hole, winning them a free game.

"Does this mean you and Jordan are friends again?" Victor asked in the car on the way home.

"No," Tara responded. "I only defended her because Jenny is an obvious idiot. That doesn't erase the fact that Jordan's lies almost broke us up." *Oops. Did I just say that? Maybe Victor didn't notice.* "Anyway, what's this about her quitting prom queen? Does she think I can't win fair and square? Well, I can. I don't need Miss Popularity's pity. If anything, she needs *mine*."

"'Broke us up?'" Victor repeated, clearly ignoring everything she'd said after that part. He swung the car into Tara's driveway, shifted into park, and faced her. "Are we, like, a couple?" he asked, sounding surprised.

"Uhhhh . . ." Tara was unable to discern if Victor was exhibiting the oh-my-God-I-was-thinking-the-same-thing surprised tone of voice or the you've-got-to-be-kidding-me-that's-ridiculous kind. So she said, ". . . Errrrr, I don't know," and wished she could curl herself into a tiny ball and roll out of the car unnoticed.

But she could feel Victor gazing at her with those sweet hazel eyes of his. She peeked at him and he drew closer. Was he going in for a kiss? Caught off guard, she tilted her head to the left instead of the right, mirroring him. And instead of the knee-weakening kiss that she'd hoped for, she received — and delivered — an awkward peck on the nostril. *The nostril!*

"Um. Heh-heh," Victor mumbled, pulling away.

"Yeah." Feeling shaken and unbelievably stupid, Tara reached blindly for the door handle. "I should go," she said, jumping out of the car. "Thanks for the flog. Golf! I mean, golf! Bye!"

Tara spun around and race-walked to her house, hardly able to believe her first date with Victor had ended so tragically.

"Put it this way: It could have happened at the prom. That'd be *way* more humiliating," Nisha offered over the phone the next morning. Tara strode down Main Street with her iPhone held to her ear. She had suppressed her desire to hide underneath her fluffy purple comforter long enough to take a trip downtown to shop for a prom dress.

"True," Tara replied, feeling somewhat better about the non-kiss action with Victor last night, though acutely aware of the slight chance it *could* happen again — *at the prom*. "I hope he realizes I'm not some weird nose freak!" she cried, which caused a woman pushing a stroller to glance in her direction. Tara shot her a weak smile and walked faster.

"I doubt he thinks that," Nisha said. "But maybe you should give it another test run, you know, before the big night? I don't want to see any nostril-love on the dance floor — unless it's on purpose."

Tara rolled her eyes. "Thanks for the advice," she replied. Actually, it wasn't a bad idea — *if* Victor was willing to kiss her again.

"Well, I've got to go," Nisha told her. "We're taking Kali and Dutta to Chicago for the day."

"Have a good time," Tara said, before ending the call. She tilted her face toward the sunshine and closed her eyes. *It's a beautiful day for a road trip,* she thought. *And for shopping — too bad I have to do it alone.*

Tara was still too embarrassed about last night to call Victor. Nisha was obviously busy. And Jordan, well . . .

Opening her eyes, Tara pressed an icon on her phone, clicking the list of stores that she planned to visit, though she wasn't sure what good it would do since she'd already been to all of them — *twice* — with Nisha and Jordan.

I guess I'll hit Macy's again. She remembered trying on a decent dress over there. Granted, it wasn't *even close* to matching Tara's high standards but it was okay, and she'd been shopping for a ridiculous amount of time. *If my perfect prom gown hasn't made itself known by now . . . well, maybe there's no such thing.*

As Tara ambled down the busy sidewalk, looking in the different store windows with their matching green-and-white awnings, she vowed to simply buy a cute dress and be done with it. *So I* won't *have a fabulous prom dress. At least I'll have an awesome date,* she thought, turning a corner.

She found herself facing the window of Timeless Treasures, a vintage clothing store that she would never dream of shopping in since Tara didn't *do* used. But there, displayed on an antique fitting mannequin, was a pale pink strapless cocktail dress. It seemed to cast a rosy hue from within as if it were magically calling for her attention.

Or maybe it was the pink light illuminating the display. Whatever.

Tara stepped closer for a better view. Tiny rhinestones bejeweled the bodice, and a filmy outer layer of tulle gave a hint of sparkle on the skirt. As if the dress wasn't perfect enough, a pretty pink satin bow adorned the waist, matching the color and texture of the dress's underskirt.

"I have to have it," she breathed.

Would it fit?

Tara nearly knocked over a boy and his puppy as she dashed into the store. "I need to try on that dress in the window," she announced to an older woman with a blond beehive, whom she assumed was the shop owner. "It's a matter of life and death!" She added that part because the woman didn't seem too thrilled about taking it down from the display. And it was also kind of true.

"It's a beauty," the woman said. "From the fifties."

Tara clasped her hands as the owner took her *sweet time* removing the gown from the window. *Come on, come on . . .* She wanted to push the lady out of the way and do it herself, but she practiced restraint. Finally, the woman placed the dress in Tara's arms and showed her to a tiny dressing room in the back.

She had barely slipped the garment over her head when the owner called, "Let me see it, baby doll. I can alter it if it's too big."

Finally, Tara emerged from the room to find the owner with a measuring tape around her neck, fiddling with a box of straight pins.

"Ohhhh," the woman murmured as soon as she caught sight of Tara.

Tara hurried across the shop to the three-way mirror, her body tingling with excitement when she observed her reflection. The satin, the sparkles, it was all . . . breathtaking! She twisted to view the stunning gown at all angles.

"Do you know what this means?" she asked the shop owner, who shook her head no. "It *means* . . . I finally found my prom dress!" Tara released an involuntary squeal, and then, with no one but the owner to hug, rushed to give the woman a giant squeeze.

"I've never seen a girl so happy about a dress," the woman said, laughing. "Have you been looking long?"

"You have no idea," Tara told her. "My two best friends . . . well, never mind. Let's just say I've been looking for a while."

She was about to say that her two best friends had found their gowns ages ago, but stopped herself. Because Tara didn't have *two* best friends anymore.

Tara entered the dressing room again, trying to focus on the sweet aspect of her bittersweet feelings. So, okay, it would have been better if her girls were there to drool over the gown with her — and to help celebrate the purchase.

But they weren't. Big deal.

At least Tara had found her special prom dress. Maybe it was time to move on to more positive things. Like accessories.

After changing back into her clothes, Tara made her way to the jewelry counter where, almost instantly, she spotted a beautiful antique necklace hanging on a hook — a Y-shape of glistening white stones and pretty pale pink pearls.

Perfect! she thought. Why was accessory shopping always waaaay easier than main-outfit shopping?

Tara carefully looped the necklace around her fingers and brought it, along with her prom dress, to the register. As the owner rang up the sale, Tara glanced around at the other things in the shop. Her gaze drifted over a glistening green-sequined flapper dress . . . an absurd houndstooth jacket with enormous shoulder pads . . . a one-shouldered silk gown with a sexy slit up the side . . .

Which looked a heck of a lot like Jordan's prom dress.

"That's a pretty number, isn't it?" the woman said, noticing that Tara was staring at it. "I've had a lot of lookers, but I doubt I'll find a buyer. It's a size six and the girl who brought it in was very tall."

Wait a sec, Tara thought. *Jordan's a size six. That couldn't really be her dress. Could it?*

As Tara handed over her mother's credit card to complete the sale, the thought kept nagging at her.

"The girl who brought it in . . . did she happen to have shoulder-length blond hair and blue eyes?" Tara asked. "Really pretty? Like, *model* pretty?"

"Yup." The woman nodded. "She had a boy's name — Gordon, I think."

More like, Jordan, Tara said silently. *What would make her sell her prom gown?*

Tara knew it could only mean one thing. For some reason Jordan wasn't going to the prom anymore.

Tara swallowed hard. *Because of me?*

till Prom . . .

CHAPTER *Six*

"This *can't* be happening," Nisha moaned the next morning. She and Tara were *supposed* to be having a nice conversation over lattes in the school courtyard. She *thought* she'd be hearing more about Tara's date with Victor.

Instead, Tara had just finished telling Nisha her theory about Jordan skipping the prom.

"This thing with Jordan has gotten way out of hand," Nisha said. "We need to do an intervention, Tara, or else the prom will turn into a total nightmare!"

Tara took a sip of her coffee. "Sorry, Nish. But you'll have to intervene alone. Jordan and I aren't speaking, remember?"

"Remember?" Nisha repeated, incredulous. "Are you kidding me? You guys won't let me forget, and you know what? I'm sooo sick of it. Can't you just kiss and make up already?" she asked. "I mean, we're not supposed to be fighting at a time like this. We're supposed to be doing girly things, like getting pedicures and trying new hairstyles. Do you guys really want to ruin all the fun of prom with your arguing?"

"Are you blaming this all on *me*?" Tara asked. "*I'm* not the one who suddenly decided not to go. Do you think it's fair that Jordan just stiffed me a hundred and fifty bucks on a limo that I already paid for because Jordan *said* that she'd chip in on it? *I* don't."

"Well . . ." Nisha was about to say that she didn't think it was fair either, but that maybe they should all sit down and talk about it . . . when Nate strolled by.

71

"Hey, girls. What's up?" he asked casually, then hesitated before adding, "Uh, Tara, can I talk to you for a minute?"

Nisha expected Tara to say no, since they were in the middle of a conversation, but instead Tara stood and told Nisha that she'd be right back.

"Okaaaaaay," Nisha murmured, a bit miffed as she watched Tara and Nate head off. She couldn't hear what they were saying, but by their body language it seemed as if they were talking about something serious. Then Nate laughed and nudged Tara with his arm before she started on her way back to Nisha.

Okay, which was it? Nisha wondered. *Serious or not?* All she knew was that it was kind of weird how Tara and Nate had become so buddy-buddy ever since he'd broken up with Jordan.

"What was that all about?" she asked Tara, hoping to get answers.

"Not much," Tara replied. "He wanted to see if I was free after school — to talk about something. Probably Jordan. Maybe he's still upset, I don't know."

Really? Nisha thought. *That's not how it looked to me.*

Tara bent to collect her leather satchel, then focused on Nisha. "Look, of course I don't want our prom to be ruined. If Jordan wants to talk, I'll listen," she said. "But she's got to make the first move — not me."

Nisha brightened. "It's a first step, Tara. A *good* first step," she said. "I'll see what I can do."

"Okay," Tara said. "See you later."

"Right." Nisha downed the last swig of her latte. As she hooked her pink backpack over her shoulder, she spotted Jordan entering the courtyard from the direction of the student parking lot. *I guess I'll have to wing it*, Nisha thought, though she'd much rather have a plan for broaching the subject of reconciliation to Jordan — especially since Jordan would have to begin the peace talks.

"Hey!" Nisha said, jogging over to join

Jordan on the path that led to the school. "So what's this I hear about your not going to the prom?" There was no time for niceties. Nisha had to get straight to the heart of the matter.

Jordan seemed surprised. "I — I was going to tell you but I didn't know how," she admitted.

"So it's true?" Nisha asked. She was hoping that it had been a misunderstanding.

Jordan nodded. "How did you find out?"

"Tara saw your dress in a consignment shop downtown," Nisha said, and Jordan replied by rolling her eyes. "Come on, Jord. It doesn't matter who found out. Tara was just as freaked about it as I was."

"Really?" Jordan asked.

No. "Of *course* she was," Nisha told her. "So what's going on?"

Jordan shrugged. "I guess I feel weird about going to the prom now that things are bad with Tara. And then there's Nate, too," she said. "I admit selling my prom dress was a bit dramatic, but it was so hard to look at it. I had to do *some*thing. Something that would make me feel like I can't turn back."

"I'm not sure you can do much to fix the situation with Nate, but you *can* do something about Tara," Nisha said, touching her friend's arm. "Talk to her, Jord. I'll bet she'll listen."

Jordan shook her head. "Why should *I* be the one to talk to *her* first, Nisha? Tara's the one who started this mess. Or at least her mouth did," she added. "And you've seen how she and Nate have been flirting lately."

That part's true. "But maybe Tara has a decent explanation," Nisha responded. "Would she really throw away ten years of friendship, just like that? The least you can do is hear her out."

Jordan blinked. "I guess . . ." she said, seeming to consider it. Then she nodded. "Fine. I'll talk to her. But only if *she* comes to *me*. There's no way I'm going to her first. I shouldn't *have* to."

"It's a beginning," Nisha told Jordan, her mind whirring. *I have to get* one *of them to make the first move*, she said silently. *And I know just how to do it!*

"How are you so sure this ridiculous scheme to get Jordan and Tara back together will work?" Brian asked Nisha at the mall the next day.

Nisha wanted to say that it was because she had a ton of experience making ridiculous schemes work but knew Brian wouldn't get it, so she told him, "I have a feeling, okay? Girl's intuition. Trust me."

She had set the plan in motion yesterday during school, first by borrowing Jordan's cell phone — claiming that the battery on her own had died — and shooting Tara a text about meeting at the food court to talk. Then she deleted the sent text from Jordan's phone.

The second stage of the plan happened at lunch when Tara had left the cafeteria to use the bathroom. Nisha swiped Tara's iPhone — since Tara would never let Nisha touch it otherwise — and sent Jordan the same text she'd sent Tara, then deleted it from Tara's phone.

Nisha knew her friends would realize that they'd both been played as soon as their meeting began. She was counting on the ice-breaking factor of the situation and hoping that since both Jordan and Tara wanted a resolution — and they were both in the same place — they'd sit down and work it out. Nisha also knew that they were capable of having a civilized discussion. But she chose the very public space of the mall just in case.

So what if the whole plan was a little *High School Musical* meets "after-school special?" As long as it worked. And it would.

"I'm getting a slice of pizza. Want one?" Brian asked.

Nisha blinked, coming back to Earth, and gazed at the people chatting and eating in the food court where she and Brian were staked out. Then she spied Jordan in line by the All Things Yogurt stand. "No time for food," she told Brian, pulling him by the hand and jumping up. "We have to hide."

They took a strategic spot behind a large potted palm. Nisha peeked around it, watching as Jordan, smoothie in hand, took a table and began to survey the food court. A moment later Tara entered. She found Jordan almost immediately and headed toward the table to join her.

"This is it," Nisha whispered to Brian, nervously gripping his hand.

Tara took a seat across from Jordan and smiled, which Nisha thought was a good sign. She watched them talk a bit, then pull out their cell phones . . .

"Okay, they're discovering the setup . . ." Nisha murmured. "Right on target . . . now they're going to laugh about it . . ."

A second later, she watched Tara roll her eyes and smile and Jordan giggle as she tossed her phone back into her bag and flipped her hair behind her shoulders.

"Wow." Brian turned to look at her. "Nisha, I had no idea you were so devious," he said with an impressed grin on his face. "You're, like, a professional setup artist."

If he only knew. "Yeah, well. I'm turning in my license right after Prom," she told him.

Brian laughed, but Nisha did not. She was serious. As soon as Prom was over she was through with all the charades. No more lying about Brian, her family . . . no more lying about *anything*. That also meant giving her honest opinion to the ladies in the dressing room at Nordstrom — *Yes, madam, that Pucci-inspired trapeze dress really* does *make you look like a circus performer* — even if it caused Nisha to lose the job she'd lined up for the summer.

"Uh-oh," Brian said.

Nisha focused back on the scene. Her heart sank when she discovered that her friends were no longer laughing.

Tara, arms folded across her chest, stared stonily at some boy's burger at the next table while Jordan gestured emphatically with her hands. Then Tara slid her chair back and stood, pointing at Jordan and saying something with venom in her eyes.

"What are they talking about?" Nisha asked her boyfriend. "Can you hear them?"

"No," Brian replied and squeezed her hand. "It doesn't look good, though."

Nisha could see that for herself. And when Tara grabbed her satchel and stormed away from the table, Nisha could tell it was all over.

Seconds later her cell phone chirped with a text message from Tara.

SOOOOOO N-O-T FUNNY!!!!!

Uh–oh. All caps. Nisha quickly texted back a "sorry." She looked at Brian. "What should

80

I do now?" she asked, then gazed back at Jordan, who was still seated at the table and frantically searching through her purse. "Should I go talk to her?" She watched Jordan pull her cell phone from her bag, then dial.

Nisha wasn't surprised to hear her phone ring a moment later. "Jordan?" she said, answering it apprehensively.

"Um, just so you know? I don't appreciate being set up like that," Jordan said icily. "Oh, and also? We met. We talked. And she's an idiot. So don't expect me to speak with her again. Because I *won't*."

"Jordan," Nisha protested. "Can't we work this out? Maybe if *I'm* there to mediate we can —"

"I *told* you," Jordan interrupted. "Forget it."

"But can't we at least *talk* about it?" Nisha asked, pressing on. "What about the prom? You're still not going?"

"The *prom*? Are you kidding me?" Jordan sighed loudly over the phone. "You know

81

what, Nisha? Forget Tara. And right now I'm so angry I don't want to talk to *you*."

Click.

What do I do now? Nisha stared at the phone in her trembling palm. *All I wanted was to bring Tara and Jordan back together. Now they're both mad at me!*

CHAPTER *Seven*

"How about this one?" Shane asked Jordan two days later. He reached for a photograph from the large pile scattered on her living room rug and handed it to her. "Can you use it for your project?"

Sitting cross-legged, Jordan held the picture carefully by its edges and gazed at the image. It was a self-portrait — a close-up of her smiling brightly into the camera. A nice shot, but she wasn't sure if it spoke to her. More important, she wasn't sure it'd speak to Mr. Davidson, her photography teacher, enough to give her a passing grade.

"Let's put this one on the side," she said, adding it to the growing heap to her right.

"Jordan?" Shane said slowly. "Don't you have to start choosing pictures if you want to get this done?"

"Tell me about it," she replied. "It's just . . . this is supposed to be an introspective. I'm supposed to include my *whole* self in this series, but every time I try it ends up looking like a jumbled mess. My pictures don't make any sense, and they need to, Shane." She sighed. "I don't know, maybe I should go out and shoot some more. Feel like going to the park?" She started to rise, but Shane pulled her back down.

"Jordan, you don't need more pictures," he told her. "All you really need is . . ."

"Love?" Jordan joked and nuzzled his neck.

Shane regarded her with a curious smile then kissed her. "That too," he said, "but for this I was thinking . . . *focus*."

"Oh. Yeah, I guess." She knew Shane had a point. Maybe Jordan had been a little scattered lately. If Tara had been given this project, she would have been all over it until it was finished. No, that wasn't true. Tara would have gotten the assignment right the first time and wouldn't need a second chance for a better grade.

Don't think about her, Jordan told herself. *Think about the project. Focus.*

"Listen, let's go through everything — see if we can work with what we have here first," he told her. "If not, then we'll grab the camera and go. Deal?"

Jordan nodded and smiled slightly. "Thanks for helping me," she said, then glanced at the intimidating mountain before her. She took a deep breath. "Okay. Let's do this."

She swept her hand across the stack, sifting through the images, stopping when she noticed a familiar photo taken of her and her friends at a party only a few weeks ago. Jordan remembered the exact moment the picture was taken. She, Nisha, and Tara had been dancing like madwomen to a cover of the old Kelly Clarkson song, "Since U Been Gone," when Jordan had slung an arm around Tara and Tara had slung an arm around Nisha. Then Jordan had held out the camera and snapped the photo.

Shane leaned closer to see it. "You guys were really rocking out. Is that the infamous Tara?" he asked, pointing to the girl with the confident smile and the pretty brown waves of hair.

"Yeah," Jordan replied, her eyes stinging at the mere mention of her name. She felt her mind wandering back to yesterday — back to their final argument at the mall.

Tara had said some cruel things to Jordan. She'd started off by calling her a selfish snob. But that hadn't hurt as much as when Tara admitted how she hated how Jordan treated people — as if they should bow down to her because she had blond hair and wore a cheerleader's uniform.

According to Tara, most people *did* bow down to Jordan, and then Jordan threw them away when she tired of them. *Do I really act that way?* Jordan had wondered. *Am I as horrible as Tara says I am?*

But then the *real* truth came out — the truth that cut Jordan long and deep. "*I hate you,*" Tara had confessed, "*I've always hated you.*"

How could I not know that she hates me? Jordan wondered. *We were best friends.*

Jordan had said some mean things, too. She'd called Tara a jealous user, a backstabber. She'd said that Tara would have zero friends if it weren't for Jordan because Tara was such a cranky witch sometimes. *But I never said that I hated her — never even thought it.*

Jordan's vision blurred as her tears began to spill. Shane wrapped her into a hug and, instinctively, she slipped her arms around his waist and hugged him back. She exhaled and melted into his chest, allowing him to comfort her.

"Maybe you should give Tara a call, try talking to her again," Shane suggested gently after a few minutes.

"You don't know the awful things she said to me," Jordan replied, pulling away to swipe at her tears. "I'm so glad we don't have to deal with her at the prom. The only thing I'm going to miss about the night is seeing Nisha. . . ." *Unless she hates me, too, and I don't know it,* Jordan said to herself. Deep down, she'd already forgiven Nisha for Monday's setup, aware that it'd been done in an effort to help. *And at least I now know the truth about Tara.*

"We should do something truly amazing on the night of the prom," Shane suggested. "So you don't have to think about it."

That sounded good to Jordan. "What do you have in mind?" she asked.

Then Shane explained that some of his friends were doing a caravan to the Punktopia band festival at the university in Springfield. It was an enormous three-day event running next Thursday, Friday, and Saturday. "They're leaving Wednesday afternoon to snag a prime campsite," he told her. "Should we go, too?"

Jordan considered it. The seniors had the day off on Wednesday to prep for the prom, as well as the rest of the week. In the Emerson High tradition, students usually took road trips to Lake Michigan after the prom, but Springfield was in the opposite direction. Which was fine by her.

"Let's do it," she agreed. Taking off to a punk festival was exciting and impulsive — just what Jordan needed to forget about the prom.

Jordan rubbed her eyes and clicked the mouse on her computer, trying desperately to ignore the rays of sun streaming through the mini-blinds on her bedroom window. Focused intently on the monitor, she slightly adjusted the complicated image on the screen.

Earlier, Shane had helped her select the strongest pictures from the photos in her living room. However, it wasn't until she'd woken up with a burst of inspiration in the middle of the night that she'd known what to do with them.

For the first time in a long while, Jordan was feeling a sense of excitement about her project — as opposed to dread — which was why she'd stayed up all night scanning and uploading her prints. Now she was using a program to design an intricate photomontage.

But something about the project was *off*. It looked more like a random assortment from her photo album than the thought-provoking composition she'd imagined.

Jordan stretched her arms and yawned. She rested her head in her hands as she gazed at the ghosted blob of images before her, wondering how to fix it.

She clicked onto a silhouette of herself in a cheerleading uniform, back-kicking with her pom-poms high overhead, and pulled it to the forefront. *Nope. It works better as the central image,* she thought, then clicked it back to where it had been.

She copied and saved her project file then began to peel apart the images. Layer after layer, she exposed pictures of Tara and Nisha. Shane. Nate. One of her mom. She found a small full-figure of Nate and a large ghosting of Shane's eyes. She uncovered the old indie theater downtown, a bird soaring underneath cottony white clouds, and a beautiful sunset that she'd once captured on film. A speed-racing Mustang, a high school graduation cap, and a college textbook were included as well — even a sparkling tiara.

No matter how many different configurations Jordan tried, though, she couldn't seem to fix her montage to resemble anything more than a collection of clutter. She glanced at the digital clock on her dresser and groaned. It was five-thirty. Her alarm would be ringing in a half hour.

Now what? I can't give up and accept the D. Maybe deleting a couple of pictures will clean it up a bit . . .

Jordan went for the mouse again, but then pulled back her hand. Mr. Davidson had given her a poor grade the first time around because he thought her project was filled with fluff. He wanted Jordan to dig deeper.

Jordan had agonized over the photo selections, making sure that each choice represented her mind-set — who she was right then and there. How could she just drag a part of herself into the trash because it didn't look cute with the other parts?

Should I leave my project alone and call it finished? Jordan wondered. She examined the chaotic blend of images on her computer screen and shook her head. *I can't. This isn't who I am. A jumbled mess?*

She didn't like the idea of it at all. In fact, if Jordan hadn't known that the introspective was about *her*, she'd have to say that the subject of the montage was seriously disturbed.

Jordan stared at the work on her screen ready to pick it apart again but, instead, she noticed something different. *This girl isn't disturbed*, she thought. *More like . . . confused. She's in between friends, boyfriends. In between high school and college. In between childhood and adulthood . . .*

I guess this is me, like it or not, Jordan realized. *Maybe I should stop trying to make it pretty.*

CHAPTER

Kissing 101: B.D.A.

Before:
1) *Perfect pillow-pucker (3 sets of 15 reps*
    per day)
2) *Invest in lip-care product of choice (gloss as*
    needed)

During:
1) *Recognize approach — meaningful gaze, jutting*
    lips, etc. (varies per boy)
2) *Reverse head tilt from target's — go typically to*
    right (pay extra attention, lefties!)
3) *Keep eyes OPEN (good aim is KEY, trust me)*

After

1) *Repeat (if desired) OR . . .*
2) *Wipe mouth (if necessary)*

"Thanks for meeting me out here, Tara," Nate said. He leaned back on the bleachers, hands resting behind his head, and gazed up at the sky. "I know I've been taking up a lot of your time."

"Oh, please. It's all good." Tara climbed to the center of the stands and sat next to him, thunking her satchel down beside her and pulling out an egg-salad sandwich that she'd grabbed from the cafeteria and some chips. "It's a beautiful day. There's no point in doing lunch inside."

Nate stared at the food. "You wouldn't want to *share*, would you?" He flashed her his brilliant smile and gazed at her with his soft brown eyes. How could Tara say no?

"Oh, all right." She split her sandwich and handed him half, even though she'd been too rushed to eat breakfast and was now starving.

"She's not only gorgeous, she's generous too," Nate said, his eyes twinkling.

Gorgeous? Tara couldn't tell if he was being serious, so she nudged him with her elbow. "Shut up," she replied, unable to hold back her grin.

Today made their third meeting of the week. She knew that Nate probably needed to get some stuff off his chest about Jordan, and quite truthfully, Tara didn't mind listening. She'd even gotten a few things off her *own* chest, since clearly she couldn't bring up the subject to Nisha anymore.

It was only a couple of days ago when Nate had listened to Tara rant and cry over her blowout with Jordan at the mall. Jordan had hurt Tara deeply by calling her a friendless backstabber, and Tara had rushed to Nate's house with a ton of questions: Had Jordan really meant what she'd said? Was Tara so unlovable that people befriended her only because she was a friend of Jordan? Tara couldn't *really* be stabbing Jordan in the back by simply speaking to him, could she?

Nate had been so sweet to hear her out. He'd assured her that none of it was true — that Jordan had only said those things to hurt Tara and that Jordan was very good at hurting people.

Tara wasn't as confident about it as Nate was, but she *did* know one thing for certain. Tara had made a huge mistake when she'd told Jordan that she hated her. Because it *wasn't* true. How could it be? They'd been best friends since second grade!

But it didn't matter if Tara had uttered the three ugly words in the heat of the moment. Now that they were out in the universe, she'd never be able to get them back.

At least she had someone to talk to about it.

The way Tara saw it, she and Nate had bonded over their respective breakups with Jordan, and Nate had morphed from being a friend's ex-boyfriend to being a friend of

97

hers. A good friend. Maybe even a lifelong friend.

So how come you never mention Victor around him?

Tara nibbled on her sandwich and pushed the nagging thought to the side. She replaced it with an image of Victor — from back when he'd revealed himself as her secret crush.

She laughed to herself, remembering the sight of him in his furry cougar mascot costume, standing right there at the bottom of the bleachers, as he'd nervously asked her to the prom. At the time Tara had been horrified by the image but now, in retrospect, she thought it was . . . *sweet*.

Then her mind abruptly shifted to that awkward peck on Victor's nostril at the end of their first date. Tara was still embarrassed by it. *Maybe I* should *talk about Victor. Nate could give me the male perspective.*

"I need your opinion about something," she piped up.

"Me, too," Nate said.

"You first," they both added at the same time and laughed.

"No, you go," Tara told him, leaning back on the row behind them.

"Okay." Nate faced her. "Well, first I want to say thanks for listening to me whine about Jordan," he told her. "You've been really cool."

"Whatever," Tara said, taking another bite of her sandwich. "No problem."

"Thanks," Nate said. "But I'm sure you don't want to hear it anymore and I'm tired of talking about her. So, I think it's time for me to *stop* it. I mean, we've got better things to do with our lives, right? We should move on. . . . *Right*?"

Tara chewed slowly as she studied Nate's face. What was he saying? That he didn't want to hang out anymore because he was done talking about Jordan? Tara felt a pang. *I guess I was wrong. I guess Nate and I aren't the good friends I thought we were.*

"Okaaaaaay," she said with a casual glance his way, not wanting to show her hurt. "So, move."

"Exactly." Nate leaned forward, and before Tara knew it his lips were pressed to hers.

Nate was kissing her!

Huh? Tara pulled away, shocked, her face flushing hotly. "Nate! What was that all about?"

"I — I thought you wanted to, Tara," Nate said. "I guess I mixed up the signals."

Signals? I wasn't giving out signals.

Sure, Tara had had the occasional daydream about Nate, and if the circumstances were different she probably *would* have wanted to kiss him. But . . .

"Nate, I'm seeing Victor. And I really like him," Tara explained. "And there's Jordan. You were her boyfriend, like, a week ago! I could never —"

She stopped when she noticed that Nate wasn't listening. Instead, he was staring at something in the distance behind her. Tara looked over her shoulder —

She gasped when she saw Victor standing by the chain-link fence that separated the bleachers from the track. Tara couldn't decipher if his expression was of hurt or anger, but she could certainly tell that he'd seen the kiss.

"Victor, let me explain," she began, her heart thudding.

Victor scoffed. He pivoted and marched back in the direction of the school.

Tara glanced at Nate, then grabbed her stuff. "Victor!" she called, maneuvering the bleachers in her platform slides. She kicked them off and raced down the path after Victor. "Please! Wait!"

Victor didn't wait or even slow his pace, so Tara pressed faster. Finally she caught up to him. "Victor," she said, clutching at his arm. "Stop . . . please. We need . . . to talk." *And I need to work out,* she realized.

Victor turned sharply. "We don't need to do *anything*," he said through gritted teeth. "I *saw* you this time. I was so stupid to think you'd want to be with a guy like me."

This time? Tara's heart dropped as she remembered the lie that Jordan had told Victor — the one about Tara and Nate kissing. "But I *do* want to be with you, Victor. This is *so* not what it looks like. I promise!"

"Don't waste your breath," Victor replied. He shook his head. "You know, people warned me about you —"

"Who? *Jordan*?" Tara broke in. "She was lying about me and Nate. It didn't happen!"

"I didn't *say* it was Jordan." Victor rolled his eyes. "You know . . . forget it. Whatever." He started away.

"Wait! What were you going to say?" Tara felt as if her heart was tearing from her chest, but she was too afraid to follow. "Victor? Won't you at least give me a chance to explain?" she asked in a voice so small it surprised her. "I know I can make you believe me."

Victor reached for the door to the school and pulled it open. "Why? So you'll still have a prom date?" he countered, not turning around.

Tara's eyes stung with tears at the sound of the words. "You mean . . . we're not going to the prom anymore?" she asked, her body trembling.

"What do *you* think?" Victor replied, then disappeared inside the building.

Tara stared after him, unable to move as she tried to process what had just occurred.

Nate came up from behind and put a hand on her shoulder. With tears now streaming down her cheeks, Tara instantly turned to him for comfort. "Oh, Nate!" she said, crying into his chest. "Victor dumped me!"

"Well, I guess *we* should go to the prom together since it looks like you don't have a date anymore," Nate said with a chuckle.

"Is that *a joke*?" Tara snapped, pulling away. She didn't see the humor.

"No, but the dude is seriously pissed," Nate replied. "You guys aren't getting back together anytime soon. That's for sure."

Tara stared at Nate, stunned, unable to believe what she was hearing. *Am I in some twisted alternate reality?* she wondered. *But maybe he's right.*

CHAPTER *Nine*

Nisha's *ghunghroos* jingled around her ankles as she stamped her bare feet in time to her *Kathak* guru's rhythmic chanting. With her arms raised overhead and a joyful expression, she spun around and around if she was gathering the warmth of the sun and sharing it with the world.

Nisha ended the dance with an enchanting smile, her emerald-green *churidar* pants swishing on her legs as she breathed heavily and glanced at Gargi Kumar for approval.

Was it okay? she wondered, feeling lucky that her guru had offered to give her private instruction. Nisha had already performed in the Todi Studio for Indian Classical Dance's end-of-year recital last Saturday so, technically, the school was closed for the summer.

"Lovely!" The guru clasped her hands, beaming at her student. "Nisha, you were simply flawless. I am so proud of you, my child." She held her arms open and Nisha jingled over for a hug.

Wow, Nisha thought. This was big — like, *major.* Guru was *not* a touchy-feely, huggy kind of woman, and in all the eleven years Nisha had been learning *Kathak,* her guru had never, *ever* told her she was flawless. Nisha had gotten compliments from her before, but it was always something like, "That was wonderful, but your hand was a bit too high during the *amad.* It needs to be lower on your hip." Or "Your *tatkars* were splendid, but your eyes were not as enchanting as they could have been. Let's see it again." But flawless? It was unheard of and such an honor — just as much, if not more, than when Guru gave Nisha her very first pair of *ghunghroos* back when Nisha was a little girl.

"Promise me that you will continue with your training when you are away in college," the guru said, sternly, when they had parted.

Nisha nodded. "Of course, Guru," she said, knowing that Emory University did not offer an Indian Classical Dance program. But she was sure she'd find one somewhere in Atlanta. Even if she couldn't, Nisha had already vowed to practice on her own. Dancing was such a part of her, she would never give it up.

"Good," the guru said, seeming somewhat satisfied. "Because a talent like yours is a gift that should not be wasted on college parties."

"Uh-huh," Nisha replied, but she was still going to attend lots of parties. She was a dancer, not a monk, for goodness sake!

"Now then, I have something that I would like to discuss with you," Guru Kumar told her. "Shall we go to my office?"

Nisha watched the petite, regal woman's long braid swish back and forth as she followed her out of the studio and across the hall to her office. After filling two hourglass-shaped cups with the tea that she always had brewing, the guru handed one cup to Nisha and sat behind a large mahogany desk.

Nisha sat on the opposite side of the desk and took a nervous sip of tea, wondering what her teacher had to say. It wasn't as if hanging out and drinking tea in her office was an everyday thing.

Finally, the guru folded her hands, placed them on the desk in front of her, and spoke. "Nisha, I would like to present an opportunity to you. I haven't had a word with your parents yet — I wasn't sure if you were ready. But after today's performance, I know now that you are."

Nisha slid to the edge of her seat, curious. "Ready for what?" she asked.

"How would you like to come to India with me to perform on the classical dance circuit? There are several important festivals this summer."

Nisha gasped. "Me?"

"Yes, *you*." Guru Kumar smiled. "Nisha, you must show the world your artistry. Perhaps one day *Kathak* might become your profession?" she said with a lilt of hope in her voice.

"Wow . . . I — I don't know what to say," Nisha replied. Of course she was thrilled that her guru considered her talented enough to become a professional *Kathak* dancer . . . but Nisha had other ideas. First, she wanted to check out Environmental Studies at Emory, then go for fashion at F.I.T., maybe combine her knowledge to design an innovative and eco-conscious line of clothing or two, *and then* become a contributing editor at *Vogue*.

Or something along those lines.

Plus going away for the summer meant that Nisha would have to give up the temp job she'd lined up at Nordstrom.

Oh, who cares about that? she decided.

Nisha *did* care, however, about her plans to spend the entire summer with Brian and her friends before they all went to separate colleges.

But this is India. It's such an amazing opportunity, Nisha thought as she imagined the scenic train rides through the beautiful countryside . . . the incredible performances. Would she get to dance on the same stage as her guru . . . *at the same time?*

"Well?" Guru Kumar asked. "What do you think? Is it something you would like to do?"

"Ummmm . . ." Nisha was torn.

On one hand, an international dance festival was something she totally wanted to experience. On the other, what would happen between Tara and Jordan this summer if Nisha left? Would the wedge grow bigger with no hope of reconciliation? And the idea of tearing herself away from Brian for so long was making her a little queasy.

". . . Can I think about it before we talk to my parents?" she asked. "I kind of had other plans."

Guru Kumar pursed her lips tightly, clearly unhappy with the response.

Thankfully, Nisha heard her cell phone ringing in the distance. Normally she wouldn't bother to answer it at the studio, but she wanted to get out from underneath her guru's disapproving stare. "Um, that's my phone. Be right back. Okay?"

Before her guru could reply, Nisha bolted through the doorway and into the small dressing room adjacent to Gargi Kumar's office. She proceeded directly to her gray mini messenger bag, slipped out her cell phone from the side pocket, and checked the caller ID. It was Tara.

"What's up?" Nisha said, answering the call. She was immediately unnerved by a loud wail followed by a fit of uncontrollable sobs. "Tara!" Nisha cried, worried. "What happened?"

"It's Victor . . ." Tara said in a shaky voice. Then she stopped, weeping.

"Tara, tell me what happened to Victor," Nisha said, her heart racing but trying to sound calm for Tara's sake. "Is he hurt?"

"He . . . he . . ." Tara said, trying to catch her breath. "He dumped me!" She burst into fresh tears.

"Oh, no!" Nisha wanted to ask how and why but decided that would all have to wait. *Tara's losing it,* she thought. *I have to go to her.*

"Where are you?" Nisha asked.

"Still at school," Tara sobbed.

"Stay where you are," Nisha ordered her. "I'm coming to get you." She hung up and immediately dialed Brian, asking him if he could pick her up. "Tara needs me," she explained, and Brian said that he would be there in a flash.

Nisha slipped off her *ghunghroos,* changing out of her *churidar* pants and matching green *choli* top, and into a pair of faded capri jeans and a black tee. She slid into her flip-flops and raced back to her guru's office.

"I'm sorry, Guru, I have to leave. It's an emergency," Nisha explained, peeking her head in from the doorway. "Thank you for asking me to go to India. I'd like to let you know by Monday, if that's okay."

Her guru nodded slightly.

Nisha thanked her again, pressed her palms together, and bowed her head as a sign of respect. Then she sprinted down the hall and burst out the front door of the Todi.

Brian was just parking his red Honda Civic in front of the studio. He spotted her and leapt out of the car at once.

Nisha ran to him, relieved that he had come so quickly. She wrapped her arms around his shoulders and hugged him tightly. "Thanks for coming," she whispered.

Brian hugged her back. "What's going on? What happened to Tara?"

"I'll tell you on the way," Nisha replied, and Brian led her to the car.

"Nisha?"

Nisha cringed at the sound of her guru's voice. She turned meekly to see the woman's surprise at the sight of Brian. Then the guru's brows furrowed, and the thin line of disapproval reappeared across her mouth.

"What did you do to make her so mad?" Brian whispered.

Nisha knew why her guru was upset. It had to do with a little kissing incident between Nisha and Brian in the Todi Studio's dressing room that her guru had witnessed a few weeks ago.

Then, Gargi Kumar had promised not to inform Nisha's parents about it — as long as Nisha ended the relationship with Brian. Nisha had agreed but, of course, she hadn't *meant* it.

Nisha stepped forward, her mind racing as she tried to formulate a logical excuse. But she knew her guru would never believe her. She also knew that, unlike the Nisha of late, Guru was a woman of her word.

"I see now why you do not want to go to India," the guru told her, a mixture of anger and disappointment darkening her eyes. "If you lied to me about breaking it off with this boy, then I gather you lied to your parents, too. It's time they learn the truth."

Several hours later, Nisha nervously twisted her long ponytail around her fingertips, hesitating outside her front door. Tara was safely home in bed, and Nisha had promised to call her after dinner. She looked over her shoulder to see that Brian was still stopped by the curb, waiting for her to go inside.

There had been no point in having him drop her off a few blocks away. Surely by now Guru had told her parents all about Nisha's secret boyfriend.

Well, I've got to face them sometime, Nisha thought. She drew in a breath and opened the door. She stepped inside and was greeted by the delicious scent of garam masala spices and the sound of laughter, both coming from the kitchen.

They don't seem upset at all, Nisha thought, hoping that meant her guru had had a change of heart about calling her parents.

"I'll bet that's Nisha," she heard Dutta comment as she slipped off her flip-flops by the front door.

"Good, now we can eat," Kali replied.

"You had better stop eating so much," her father laughed. "You're going to get fat."

"Oh, don't worry. I'll be fat soon enough anyway!" Kali said.

Nisha paused, her heart jumping as she forgot about her problems for a second. *Is she saying what I think she's saying?*

A moment later her father raced into the foyer. "Nisha! Come quickly. Your sister has some exciting news!"

Nisha hurried into the kitchen with her father. "Are you . . . ?" she asked Kali, and her sister nodded.

"We're having a baby!" Dutta cried, his cheeks red.

"We were looking for the right time to spring it on you," Kali added with a smile. "I guess it's now."

"Congratulations!" Nisha rushed to hug her sister, then Dutta. "Oh, my gosh. I can't believe I'm going to be an aunt!"

"Here, *Beta*," Mrs. Khubani said, handing Kali a piece of unleavened bread. "Have some *roti*. You are eating for two now."

The whole family laughed and talked, exhilarated by the great news. While Dutta and her father chatted, Nisha and her mom tried to explain how to make a *gobi* vegetable dish to Kali since she thought it important for her to overcome her cooking challenges *right then*.

When the phone rang, Nisha didn't think anything of it. *It's probably Tara or maybe Jordan*, she thought, watching her mom answer it.

"Oh, hello, Gargi," her mother said brightly into the receiver. "Do you need to speak with Nisha?"

Nisha froze when her heard her guru's

name. She swallowed hard when her mother glanced her way.

"No, I did *not* know," Mrs. Khubani said. "Is that right? . . . At the studio? . . . With *whom*?"

Tiny beads of perspiration formed on Nisha's forehead. She clenched her hands as she watched her mother's expression change from pleasure . . . to puzzled . . . to *really peeved*.

Nisha knew she was in big trouble when, after hanging up the phone, her mother asked her father to step out of the kitchen so that they could talk in private.

Oh, God. Nisha's stomach churned as she watched them leave without so much as a glance in her direction. Kali and Dutta had just enough time to give Nisha a sympathetic look before her parents returned and asked the couple to leave the kitchen so they could speak with Nisha alone.

Trembling, Nisha shrank into her seat, waiting for her parents to blast her.

"Who is this Brian?" her mother began. "You know we do not approve of dating."

"I know, but —"

"What kind of boy would go out with a girl and not want to meet her parents?" Nisha's father added.

"Well, actually he *does* want —"

"How will poor Raj feel when he finds out?" Mrs. Khubani countered. "He will be devastated, that's how!"

Nisha bit her tongue, resisting the urge to tell them that good ol' Raj had a honey waiting for him back at the Sorbonne in Paris. Instead she said, "Maybe I *wouldn't* have lied if you guys would have been even *a little* reasonable! I'm seventeen!" she cried. "People my age have boyfriends — they go out on dates! I just want to go to *the prom* with my *boyfriend*! There's nothing *wrong* with that!"

Nisha pulled back when she saw her father's face turn a deep shade of purple. He looked as if he were about to pop a blood vessel. "Dad, I'm sorry. I didn't mean to be so —"

Mr. Khubani held up a hand to silence her. Her father was quiet now — which cautioned Nisha to tread lightly or risk making the situation worse.

"Whether you think you should be dating or not is of no importance," he said, quietly seething. "The fact remains that you — our youngest daughter — have been lying to us for a very long time."

"Who knows what other lies she's told?" her mother added, nodding at him and then at Nisha.

"And for that, there are consequences, Nisha." Her father took a step forward and rested his palms on the kitchen table. "So you will *not* be going to the prom with Raj *or* with Brian or with *anybody* . . . because you are *grounded*."

*1 day and 1 minute
till Prom . . .*

CHAPTER *Ten*

Random To-Dos

1) *Sched. mani/pedi (for 1)*
2) *Hair appt. (up? down? half up/half down?)*
3) *Rhinestone sandals vs. pink satin heels?*
4) *Call limo place 2 pkup @ N's house 1st
   (cancel V's)*
5) *Buy waterproof mascara*
6) *Boutonniere?*
7) *Smile! (a real one)*

This is so *not how I pictured the pre-prom-extreme-makeover extravaganza,* Tara thought as she exited the salon — *alone.* She had just spent the last hour-and-a-half getting buffed, waxed, plucked, and polished for the big day tomorrow.

Sure, her skin was looking luminous, and her fingers and toes shimmered with the prettiest pale pink polish ever, but what was the fun of getting beautified if you had nobody to share the experience with?

Tara had expected to spend the momentous occasion with Nisha — *who's grounded* — and Jordan — *who hates my guts* — filled with tons of laughter and gossip and silly picture-taking.

Feeling glum and trying not to smudge her toenail polish, she waddled back to her car in her white flip-flops. No après-salon latte with the girls. No giddy chatter about the big night ahead. As a matter of fact, Tara had nothing left to do but head to the Fairmont Hotel to check out the venue one last time before the prom.

Her cell phone rang just as she was about to hop into her car; Nate's picture popped up onto the screen.

"Hey," Nate said when she answered. "I'm at the florist. What kind of corsage do you want?"

He's asking me *what kind of gift he should buy me?* Tara thought, bewildered.

Nate had spent the entire weekend trying to convince her to attend the prom with him, his argument being that he didn't have a date because Jordan dumped him and she didn't have one because Victor dumped her. So they might as well go together.

Tara had felt very weird about it at first. Several failed attempts to speak with Victor had left her completely devastated. But after a couple of days, and some clarity, she started to get annoyed. Tara wasn't guilty of any wrongdoing, and if Victor couldn't give her the *common courtesy* of hearing her out then why *shouldn't* she go to the prom with Nate?

After all the hard work she'd put into the prom, Tara *deserved* to have a good time. And it wasn't as if Jordan and her

I-own-every-cute-boy-at-Emerson-High
attitude would be there.

Speaking of cute boys, maybe Nate
needed a little help with the rules of corsage-
ment. "It kind of takes all the fun out of
getting one if I have to pick it out myself,
don't you think?" she asked sweetly.

"Okay. I'll just choose one then," Nate
replied. He was about to hang up when Tara
thought of something.

"Wait! Don't get one that will clash
with my dress," she suggested. "I'm wearing pink."

"Okay."

"Oh, and I'm not into carnations . . . or
baby's breath . . . or the colors orange, black,
or teal — for flowers, that is. Peonies are
nice, though."

"Anything else?" Nate asked.

"Nope. That's it — just keep the foliage
to a minimum. But I'm sure I'll like anything you pick out. Thanks!"

Tara clicked END and checked the time
on her phone. Then she headed to the

Fairmont, where, just as she'd expected, the setup was running smoothly. At the moment, the walls were being bathed in silver and blue tulle and the bare tables were already in position around the dance floor.

"Did you say you wanted the disco ball?" the manager of the hotel asked her.

"Absolutely," Tara replied. "It's not a party without one." She checked the list on her iPhone. "The ice sculpture should be arriving late tomorrow. Just put it off to the side by the punch bowl," she informed him, then glanced around. "I think that's it. Everything looks great so far. Call me if you have any questions."

"Will do," the manager said and escorted her to the door of the ballroom.

Feeling as if a weight was suddenly lifted off her shoulders, Tara breezed down the hallway and into the lobby, where she noticed that a large delivery was being carried into the hotel. *How come they're not using the service entrance?* she wondered. *Whatever. At least they're delivering it today and not tomorrow.*

Tara passed by the two burly deliverymen, glancing at the tall crates positioned in the center of the lobby.

"Hey, miss. Do these things look in line with the entrance to you?" the guy with a mustache asked her.

Tara checked it. "I think so," she said, wondering what could possibly be inside the boxes. Quite frankly she was a bit worried since it was the first thing her prom guests would see when they entered the hotel. "What *is* all this stuff?" she asked, gesturing to the delivery.

"Oh, just some junk for a prom," the deliveryman said.

Prom? As in the Emerson prom? Tara thought with a sinking feeling. Then the second delivery guy pulled open a crate to reveal —

"Snow White!" Suddenly dizzy, Tara gasped for air. She grabbed hold of one of the smaller crates to steady herself — one of the *seven* smaller crates, she realized. "There wouldn't happen to be a bunch of dwarfs in these boxes, would there?"

"Why, yes, there would," the man replied with a smirk, clearly registering Tara's horror. "Snow's supposed to hold a sign directing the kids to the big bash." He handed her the purchase order. "See?"

Tara scanned the yellow paper. At the bottom was Jenny Brigger's signature. *What a shocker,* she thought. *So, this is her awesome prom surprise. First I have a fight with Jordan, then I break up with Victor, and now this? I am so* sick *of surprises!*

Tara wanted to scream. She had fought Jenny tooth and nail to turn their "Once Upon a Time" prom into an elegant affair. And she wasn't about to let the girl cheese it up with her sick storybook obsession.

"Pack it up, buddy," she told the guy who had just opened another box, revealing Dopey's irritating grin. "We're moving these babies out of here."

"And who are *you*?" the guy asked.

"I'm Tara Macmillan, chairwoman of the Emerson High School prom committee," she replied, her hands on her hips. "And what I say goes, got it?"

The man shrugged. "Just sign right here," he told her, pointing to a blank line on the purchase order, and Tara did. "Where to?" he asked.

"Where they belong," Tara replied. "In the basement." *Let's see if Jenny likes* my *surprise.*

I can't believe the prom is really here, Tara said to herself the next evening in her room as she studied her image in the full-length mirror. Her brown wavy tresses were pulled into an elegant French twist with her bangs swept lightly to the side. Tara loved her pink strapless dress and her Y-shaped necklace even more today than when she'd first discovered them, and the rhinestone strappy heels she'd found to match were killer.

She took a fluffy blush brush off her dresser and dipped it into a pot of loose pink powder. *You are going to have a good time tonight*, Tara thought, psyching herself up. *Even if things aren't exactly how you wanted them to turn out. Right?*

From the very start Tara had been wrong about all things Prom — what theme the party would have, what kind of dress she'd wear, even who would be her date. Some things had worked out anyway and some things definitely had not.

Tara could deal with all that, but being wrong about her friends? That one was tougher. *It's not supposed to be like this. I thought we'd all be together on this day. Getting ready for Prom is supposed to be fun, not lonely.*

As Tara highlighted each cheek with a swipe of blush, she heard a car pull up to the front of the house. She peeked out from her second-floor window to see that her date had arrived.

The back door of a black limousine opened and Tara felt her stomach flutter. Nate Lombardo stepped out in a classic black tuxedo and walked confidently up the path to the house. His sandy-brown hair was cutely tousled. They had agreed to attend the prom as friends but that didn't mean he wasn't still adorable.

It was then that Tara wondered what Victor would have looked like walking up the path to pick her up. *Stop thinking about him,* she scolded herself.

"Tara! Your date is here!" she heard her dad holler up the stairs.

"Coming!" Tara called. She gave a final twirl before the mirror, grabbed her new shimmering silver clutch from the bed, and set off downstairs.

She found her mom at the bottom of the steps with a video camera practically glued to her right eye. "Oh, Hal, isn't she pretty?" Mrs. Macmillan cooed, capturing Tara descending the last three steps.

"My little princess . . ." Tara's dad said and wistfully snapped a picture. "She's grown up into a lovely young lady. How did this *happen,* Trish?"

"Daaad." Tara glanced at Nate, embarrassed.

"He's right," Nate said, nodding up at Tara. "You look beautiful."

"Thanks. You, too. I mean, handsome," she said. Why was she suddenly nervous? Then there was an awkward moment when she had trouble pinning the boutonniere she'd bought — a single pink rose to match her dress — onto Nate's lapel, all while her dad snapped photos.

"I left your corsage in the limo," Nate admitted. "Do you want me to get it?"

"No, I can put it on later." She turned her head slightly to glimpse her mom, who was now getting rather creative with the camera, obtaining shots from several angles. "I think it's time to go," she whispered to Nate.

"Wait, we need some footage by the limo," her mom said, and Tara turned beet red.

Her parents videotaped them walking down the path and then made them pose for pictures by the car. It was all so surreal.

She was taking prom photos with Jordan's boyfriend. Her face hurt from pretending to smile. Finally, the driver opened the back door and Tara climbed inside the luxurious cabin and Nate slid in next to her.

Hmmm. Not bad. Satellite radio, TV and DVD combo, glossy minibar stocked with . . . She opened it. *Sodas.*

"Okay, bye!" she called to her parents.

Mr. Macmillan took one last photo before leaning into the open window and saying, "I want her home by midnight, Nate. She may be a young woman, but she'll always be my little princess. You get my drift?"

Nate swallowed. "Uh, yes, sir," he said as Tara hid her face with a hand, mortified. *Why do my parents have to be such dorks?*

When they were finally on their way, Tara sank into the cushiony leather and exhaled. "Sorry about my parents."

"Nah, it's cool. Mine are the same way. Notice how we're conveniently forgetting to stop at my house en route to the prom?" he said as he removed a clear plastic box from the shelf by the back window. He showed it to her. Inside was a single dark pink peony pinned to a silver elastic band. "I hope you like your corsage."

"Nate, it's gorgeous!" Tara gasped and held out her right wrist for him to slip it on. "How did you know I love peonies?"

"You told me!" Nate said, laughing.

Tara tilted her head. "Really?" *Who knew Nate was so attentive?*

Nate flicked on the radio and played with the digital tuner until he found a song with a decent beat. Curious about the buttons on the panel to her left, Tara pressed one. The sunroof above them slid open. She glanced up at the blue sky, the sun still shining bright, and then shot Nate a devilish grin.

"Want to stand up?" she asked. "I've never done it before — probably because this is my first time in a limo — but I've always wanted to."

"Sure," Nate said and helped her to her feet.

Tara stood carefully on the seat and popped out from the top of the roof. She raised her arms over her head, loving the feeling of wind on her skin as the limousine cruised through the suburban streets of Selina.

A minute later, Nate squeezed in by her side wearing a pair of aviator shades. "Always prepared. Former Boy Scout," he explained and casually slipped an arm around her waist as if he'd done it a million times before.

It seemed like the natural thing to do, but Tara's muscles tensed and she lowered her arms. Hadn't they agreed to go to the prom as friends? "Um . . ."

"Don't you think it's kind of romantic up here?" Nate asked, a smile spreading across his chiseled face.

But Tara had to look away. Yes, wearing a stunning gown and watching the world go by from the sunroof of a limousine with your fantasy date — who seemed really into you, by the way — was *very* romantic. And a few weeks ago she might have dropped dead from happiness at a moment like this, but now?

Now it only made her think of Victor.

And Jordan.

"Nate? We're *friends,* remember?" Tara said.

"Right. Okay." He removed his arm. "But you never know where the night will lead us," he added hopefully and wiggled his eyebrows to make her laugh.

The driver pulled up in front of the Fairmont, and it was all Tara could do to wait for Nate to walk around the car and open the door. She was dying to see what the ballroom looked like!

Nate grabbed her hand as they breezed up the steps and through the elegant lobby, which was lacking a certain gaudy display, thank goodness. Clearly Jenny hadn't arrived yet, because if she had, Tara was certain that she'd be waiting for her by the front steps, ready to pounce.

When they reached the entrance to the ballroom, Tara hesitated, letting a gaggle of chatty girls in filmy dresses enter first. It was the moment of truth. Had the "Once Upon a Time" theme turned out elegant . . . or tacky?

She could hear the band playing classic Bob Marley, which she thought was a good sign because who didn't like Bob Marley, right?

Finally Tara and Nate stepped inside, and Tara's lips parted in a smile as she looked around. The room was draped in pretty silver and baby blue tulle with the tables covered in matching linens. Vases brimming with cream-colored tulips were the centerpieces. Off to her left, a photographer was snapping keepsake photos of happy couples in front of a backdrop that looked like a storybook. It was going to be a sit-down dinner so there were no buffet stations, but there was a table at the back of the room boasting bowls of cherry punch and hors d'oeuvres.

The gleaming wooden dance floor was empty, but Tara had a feeling that it wouldn't be long before it was packed with Emerson students showing off their moves.

"Oh, Nate. Isn't the room glamorous?" Tara cried, taking it all in.

"Yeah, looks great," Nate said, nodding.

"Naaaaaaate!" someone called.

Tara and Nate whipped around to find Moose, the burly catcher from the baseball team, waving enthusiastically at them.

"Moooooooose!" Nate yelled back, double pointing at the guy. He turned to Tara. "Want to go say hi?" he asked.

Apparently Moose and some other boys from the baseball and football teams were causing a commotion at the far end of the room. They were greeting each other by jumping up and ramming their chests together, while their dates looked on with horror.

Tara giggled and waved to Moose.

"Actually, I've got to check on something," she replied. "I'll meet up with you in a few, okay?"

"I'll come find you," Nate said, and Tara cruised over to the hors d'oeuvres table for a closer look. She pulled the dipper out of a large crystal punch bowl and poured some cherry punch into a cup as she checked out the spread. Jalapeño poppers, tiny egg rolls, chicken skewers, brochettes, olives, hummus, pita and crackers, fruit and cheeses . . . Everything was beautifully arranged around the castle-shaped ice sculpture — which Tara and Jenny had compromised on as a display piece. It was perfect.

Punch in hand, Tara turned away from the table, satisfied. She watched her fellow students all dressed up and chatting excitedly with their friends. Then the lights dimmed and the music switched from reggae to sultry rhythm and blues. Several couples crossed onto the dance floor for some predinner dancing as the disco ball began to spin and swirl glimmering stars of light around the room.

"The whole *party* is perfect," Tara murmured. "All my hard work paid off." *And Victor's, too,* she added silently.

Tara scanned the room, wondering if he was there and feeling disappointed when she couldn't find him. *Victor probably isn't coming, and I guess I don't blame him,* she thought. *Not after he saw Nate kiss me. I just wish he would have given me a chance to explain. . . . On second thought, I wish that Nate had never kissed me at all.*

Tara knew that none of this was Nate's fault, but if he hadn't kissed her then maybe she'd still be friends with Jordan and maybe her romance with Victor wouldn't have ended before it had a chance to truly begin.

"Hey, babe. Did you miss me?" Nate said, startling Tara out of her thoughts. He slung his arm heavily around her shoulders, almost spilling her punch.

Tara felt a flash of anger. "What's your problem?" she asked hotly.

Nate seemed surprised and . . . was that a little hurt she saw in his eyes? "I'm sorry," he said, glancing away. "It's just, look, Tara — I kind of always had a little crush on you when I was seeing Jordan. And I know you liked me, too."

"How?" Tara asked. She hadn't been *that* obvious, had she?

Nate looked back at her and gave a weak grin and a shrug that let her know that she had.

"Oh, my God," she said, turning away from him. She placed her punch on the buffet and covered her face with her hands. "I feel so stupid."

"No, don't," Nate said, stepping closer and removing her hands from her face. He gazed into her eyes. "I thought maybe Prom could be, you know, the start of something. What do you think? We'd have an awesome summer together. Wouldn't we?"

Tara's mind whirled, barely able to process what Nate had just offered. *Am I hearing right? Did he just ask me to be his girlfriend?*

CHAPTER *Eleven*

"Nisha, are you coming with us to the Dixits' house for dinner or not?" Mrs. Khubani called up from the foyer.

Nisha sat up in bed. *Is she serious? Go to Raj's house on the night I'm supposed to be going to the prom with Brian?* she thought, incredulous. *I'd rather swallow an entire mouthful of chili paste.*

"Not!" she yelled back.

"Suit yourself," her mother said. "Then you can stay home."

"Fine by me," Nisha muttered and flopped back onto her mattress. She rolled onto her stomach, grabbed her cell phone off her nightstand, and speed dialed Brian's number.

"Hey," Brian said, answering.

"Hey. Are you there yet?" Nisha asked him.

"No. The limo's outside, but I was thinking about blowing the whole thing off. It's too weird going to the prom without you, Nisha," he said.

"But you *have* to go," Nisha told him. "I'd feel awful if you didn't, and who's going to take tons of pictures and then later describe every detail of the prom so that it feels like I was actually there?"

"Me?" Brian said.

"Uh-huh," Nisha replied. "Please go, Brian. I don't want you to miss out on the party of the century because I had to get myself grounded at the last minute."

She'd neglected to tell him *why* she'd gotten grounded. Did he really need to know more than that she'd snapped at her father and missing the prom was punishment for being disrespectful?

"All right, I'll go," Brian conceded. "How about I call you with a play-by-play? This way, you *will* be there with me. Sort of."

"That sounds awesome," Nisha said. "I'll be here waiting for your call." *Where else would I be?* she thought as she hung up. She paused, then decided to give Tara a quick buzz. But Tara's phone went straight to voice mail, so Nisha left a message reminding her friend to take lots of pictures, too.

Now what? Nisha wondered, tossing the phone onto the bed. Outside she heard the family car pull out of the driveway. Still on her stomach, Nisha gazed at the pretty lemon-colored prom dress hanging on the back of her closet door. She lifted herself off the bed and crossed the room to the dress. *I was almost there,* she thought, running her hand across the soft chiffon of the skirt, then to the delicate bows on the spaghetti straps.

Nisha felt the sting of tears behind her eyes and squeezed her lids closed to keep them at bay. But it was no use. *How could I have been so careless? How could I have let my guru see me with Brian?* Nisha wondered, salty drops slipping down her cheeks. *Now I'm going to miss seeing him in a tuxedo and riding to the prom in a limo and dancing every slow dance with him.*

All I wanted was one last romantic date with my boyfriend! Nisha wanted to stand on her rooftop and scream it to the world, even if she knew the statement wasn't entirely true. Because Nisha wanted more than that.

She wanted her relationship with Brian out in the open — and now it was — but she also wanted her parents to be okay with her dating him — and they weren't. *They'd never accept my dating anybody they couldn't handpick.*

Nisha wiped at her tears as she turned away from the dress to head back for the comfort of her bed. Missing the prom would probably be easier from underneath the covers, she decided.

The aquamarine sari and matching *choli*

that Kali had given her caught her eye as it rested lightly on the back of her computer chair. Nisha pulled it off the chair, accidentally unraveling the silk to the floor, as she heard a light rap on her bedroom door.

"Nisha? Are you okay in there?" Kali asked gently. "I stayed behind in case you needed to talk. Can I come in?"

"Just a minute." Still upset, Nisha quickly blotted her face with the edge of silk still in her hands. "Okay, come on in."

Kali opened the door slowly and entered the room. "Hey." She approached and wiped away a few stray tears from Nisha's cheeks. Clearly ignoring the obvious, she looked at the silk her sister was holding. "Whatcha doing?"

"Just looking at it," Nisha said. "I was going to try to figure out how it works. The last time I wore a sari was at your wedding, but I didn't wrap it myself. Mom did."

"Well, I can show you. It goes something like this." Kali grasped the silk, tucking an end into the waist of Nisha's jeans so that

145

the lower part slightly grazed the floor. She wrapped the fabric snugly around her sister once, creating a skirt. Then she carefully gathered the material into nine large pleats, tucking them into the front of Nisha's jeans as well. Kali swathed the remaining silk around Nisha once more, this time bringing it up under Nisha's right arm, draping it over Nisha's T-shirt, and allowing the rest to fall elegantly over her left shoulder. Kali stepped back to inspect her work, then led Nisha to the mirror. "Is it me or do you look good in everything?" she asked, slipping the elastic ponytail holder out of Nisha's hair, letting her long wavy tresses run free.

Nisha rolled her eyes at her sister before regarding her reflection in the mirror. Flowing with aquamarine curves, the sari *did* seem to suit her. Nisha wasn't surprised by that — she wore exotic *lahengas* for her *Kathak* recitals all the time, so why wouldn't she think a sari would look good?

Nisha *was*, however, stunned by *how* good it looked. The brilliant color of the sari made her curls seem shinier and gave her skin an unexpected radiance, which made her think that this color might have been a better option for her prom dress. Not that it mattered anymore, anyway.

She grasped the silk draped over her shoulder and drew it forward for closer inspection. For the first time, Nisha observed that the fabric had a fine gold thread running through it, creating an intricate pattern that only the wearer would ever notice.

"Kali, do you remember when I asked Mom why she still wears a sari even though we've lived in America for so long?" Nisha asked.

Kali nodded. "She said that once a woman has known the luxury of silk against the skin and the quality of true craftsmanship, she can never wear anything other than a sari."

"Mom wears it for herself," Nisha added, nodding. "To feel beautiful. It's a part of her that she's not willing to give up even if some people in this country think it's strange. She doesn't care."

"Yeah," Kali agreed. "I never thought about it that way. Go, Mom."

"Yeah." Nisha felt the cool silk between her fingers. "This is a part of me, too," she mused aloud. "A part that I love and appreciate. To me, this is India. It's just . . ." She turned to face her sister. "It's not the only part, Kali. I wish Mom and Dad could understand that." Tears began to well in her eyes again.

"Ohhhh, Nisha." Kali pulled her sister into her arms, holding her tightly as she sobbed. "I don't know if they'll ever fully understand."

"I want to please them — I really do — but no matter how much they want me to be a traditional Indian girl, I'm not. I'm part American, too." Nisha gulped for air. "Maybe I'll end up with a boy that they introduce me to — or maybe I'll marry Brian or someone else. I don't know." She pulled away from her sister. "But *I* have to be the one who determines my future. *Me.*"

"So what do *you* want for yourself?" Kali asked, snatching a tissue from the box on the nightstand and handing it to Nisha.

"I'm still trying to figure that out," Nisha admitted, patting her eyes dry. "But I *do* know one thing. I know what I want right now, at this very moment."

"What?" Kali asked.

"I want to be at the prom with Brian," Nisha replied, earnestly.

Kali studied the seriousness of Nisha's face. "Then you should go," she replied.

"Really?" Nisha asked. "Just like that? Even though I'm grounded?" Even Kali had never attempted something like that.

Kali nodded. "You shouldn't miss your senior prom," she said. "I'll cover for you if I have to."

Go to the prom? Nisha's heart pounded at the thought of it. *I could surprise Brian and he'd totally freak!* But then Nisha realized something else. "How am I supposed to get there? Mom always takes her car keys with her wherever she goes and I'm *not* about to hot-wire it."

"*Borrowing* is one thing. Grand theft auto? Not a good idea," Kali agreed. "What about your friends?"

"Well, I'm sure Tara's already *at* the prom," she said, pondering the problem, "and Jordan's probably on the road to that punk festival with Shane by now. Plus there's the fact that she's mad at me for setting up the reunion with Tara at the mall."

"Maybe Jordan hasn't left yet," Kali said.

"Maybe," Nisha replied. *But is Jordan so angry that she wouldn't help a friend in need?* she wondered.

There was only one way to find out.

CHAPTER *Twelve*

"Yes, Mom. I have my hands-free headset on. I know, cell phones and driving don't mix," Jordan droned over the phone from the driver's seat of her SUV. "And I'll call you from the rest stops . . . and when we get there . . . and at least once a day . . . and I'll ditch the campsite for a motel room if it rains. Okay?"

"Okay," her mom replied, though she sounded unsure. "Have a good time, but *be careful*."

"I will. Bye!" Jordan shook her head and smiled as she ended the call. The *fourth* call, and Jordan was still within a three-block radius of her house. Her mother was such a worrier. The Punktopia festival was in Springfield, not Timbuktu.

Jordan turned the corner onto Shane's street to find two cars parked in front of his house. Shane was leaning on the second one, talking to his friends Apollo and Gavin, and two girls and a guy that she didn't recognize.

Jordan waved at them as she parked and hurried out of the SUV. "Hey, guys," she said, leaning on the car next to Shane.

Apollo and Gavin greeted Jordan, and Shane introduced her to the others — Sophie, her sister Caitlyn, and Caitlyn's boyfriend, Mark, who were all clearly anxious to start the trip.

"We're waiting for El to come out of the bathroom," Gavin said. "Dude, how long has she been in there — two, three hours?" he asked Shane.

Then Jordan noticed the door to Shane's house open. Her stomach dropped when she saw a petite girl with short burgundy hair and heavy eyeliner emerge. The girl strode down the front path wearing a black tank, a cutoff denim mini, with ripped fishnets and platform boots.

Jordan had met this girl once before, but had never caught her name. She was the lead singer of the Violent Kittens, a punk band that Shane used to play with when he lived in Chicago. More important, she was Shane's bitter ex-girlfriend and hardly a fan of Jordan's.

The girl spotted Jordan and immediately rolled her eyes. Jordan wasn't thrilled about Miss Kitty being there either, but she was determined to be civil.

"So, your name is Elle? Like the magazine?" she asked her. "That's cute."

"Cute? I don't think so." The girl smirked. "El is short for *Elvira*. As in, the mistress of the dark?" She gave Jordan's jeans and white tee the once over. "You're wearing *that* to a punk festival?"

Jordan smirked back. *So much for civil.* "The festival starts tomorrow. So I guess you're wearing *that* camping?" She snorted. "Good luck, your majesty."

"Well, let's hit the highway," Shane said, rubbing his hands together.

El seemed miffed when Shane, Gavin, and Apollo headed for Jordan's SUV. "Doesn't anybody want to ride with me?" she asked. "Shane?"

"I will!" Apollo piped up. "Wish me luck, dude," he whispered to Gavin, then jogged over to El's car.

"Let's get this show on the road. Yeah!" Gavin yelped and leapt into the backseat of Jordan's car. "I hope you have something better than Shakira to listen to," he added.

"How about a little Rancid?" Jordan asked, getting into the car. "Good enough?"

"Classic," Gavin said, nodding. "The prom queen's taste in tunes is getting better," he told Shane.

"Sorry, I'm no prom queen," she said. "My prom is tonight. I actually have to show up to win the title, don't I?"

Shane found the band on Jordan's iPod and soon the sound of guitars thrashed through the speakers. Gavin bopped his head in the backseat and Jordan glanced at Shane and smiled.

They'd been driving for about an hour when Jordan's phone rang.

"That's probably my mother *again*," Jordan told Shane. "I'll bet she's testing to see if I'll pick the phone. She doesn't like me to use it too much while I'm driving. Do you mind answering it?" She passed her cell phone to Shane.

"Hello?" Shane asked, and then his brow furrowed. "Nisha? Well, she's driving right now. What's the matter?"

Nisha? "Something's wrong?" Jordan asked Shane, worried, but trying to focus on the road.

"Okay, slow down," Shane said to Nisha. "Wait. Hold on." He turned to Jordan. "I think you'd better take this," he said.

Jordan spotted a sign for a rest stop two miles ahead. "Tell her I'll call her back in five minutes. Then call the other cars to let them know we're getting off at the rest stop."

As Shane did that, Jordan maneuvered the car off the highway and into a spot in front of a visitor's center. The two other cars followed suit.

"We're here?" Gavin said, rubbing his eyes. Apparently, the guy had fallen asleep.

"No, dude. Rest stop," Shane said as Jordan took her cell phone from him and dialed Nisha's number.

"What happened? Nisha, are you okay?" Jordan asked the moment she heard her friend's voice. Shane and Gavin exited the car to talk to the others as Jordan listened to Nisha's story. About how her parents found out about Brian and grounded her. And how Nisha needed a way to get to the prom because she knew it could be the last date she would ever have with him.

"Brian needs to know how much I love him before my parents separate us forever,"

Nisha said. "I know you were looking forward to this concert thing, and that you're upset with me and all. But I really need you, Jord. Will you help me?"

Jordan glanced at Shane through the windshield. He was now chatting with Miss Kitty, who'd be more than happy to spend the weekend with Shane and *without* Jordan. Still, Jordan didn't have to think before responding. "Of course I'll help you." She paused before adding. "And Nisha? Don't worry about the little reunion with Tara at the mall. I'm *so* over it. I know your heart was in the right place. You couldn't have known it would end so badly." *But could she have known the truth about how Tara hates me?* she wondered. *Possibly.*

"Jordan . . ." Nisha began.

"Hey, why are you wasting time talking to *me*?" Jordan broke in with a cheerful tone. Now was not the time to get into it about Tara. "You've got to get ready for the prom! Get that dress on, Nisha. I'll be there as soon as I can."

"Thanks, Jord. You're the best!" Nisha exclaimed before saying good-bye.

Then Jordan flipped her phone closed, got out of the car, and headed over to the rest of the group. "It looks like I have to turn back, guys," she told them.

"Aw, that's too bad, *Jaden*," El said with extra sarcasm. "Don't worry, Shane, there's always room for you in my car."

She'll probably offer to make room for him in her tent, too, Jordan thought, but she trusted him. "Shane, can I talk to you for a sec?" she asked.

"Sure," he said, and they stepped a few feet away.

"I'm sorry I can't go to the festival with you. I really want to, but this is important," she told him. "It's for Nisha."

"I know it is." Shane took her hands in his. "It's just . . ."

"What?" Jordan prompted him. "Tell me."

Shane hesitated then said, "Do you really have to go? I mean, I suggested this thing so that you could forget about the prom. And we've been psyched about it for days and now you say you're *leaving*? What about *our* plans?"

Jordan couldn't tell if Shane was upset or irritated. Either way, all she could do was apologize again. "I know. It's a sucky thing to do," she said. "Really. But I *have* to go, Shane. Nisha's my best friend. She'd totally do the same for me if *I* needed *her*. Please don't be mad at me."

"Fine. Then I'm not," Shane said curtly. He dropped her hands, preferring to look at his black high-tops rather than at Jordan.

Yeah, right. He's totally mad. "Are you *sure*?" Jordan bent over, trying to make contact with his gaze *and* to make him smile. But he didn't.

"Look, I *said* I was. Okay?" Shane snapped. "What else do you want?"

Jordan sprang upright, surprised at his tone. She knew that he was disappointed but he didn't have to be rude. She glanced at the clock on her cell phone. "You know what? I should probably get going," she said, backing away. The last thing Jordan needed was to get into a last-minute argument with her boyfriend. "I'll see you when you get home and you can tell me all about the festival. Okay?" She smiled at him, then waved to the others. "Have a good time without me!" she called.

And when she turned to head back to her car, she thought she heard Shane murmur, "I will."

Jordan tried to clear her mind during the hour drive to Selina, but she kept going back and forth between feeling slighted at Shane's lack of understanding about the situation and thinking that maybe he'd had a right to be annoyed about her totally leaving him.

By the time Jordan had arrived in front of Nisha's house she had resolved to drop off her friend at the prom then swing back to Springfield in the morning to surprise Shane. If she got an early start she'd arrive in time to catch most of the music, and it would show Shane that he was important to her.

Before Jordan had a chance to push the gear into park, Nisha came rushing out the door, wearing her shimmering yellow prom gown, a pair of bronze-colored strappy heels, and the silver heart-shaped charm bracelet that Brian had given her for their six-month anniversary. The top part of her hair was pinned high, while the rest fell into thick, shiny ringlets down her back.

"Do I look okay?" Nisha asked, sliding into the car and slipping her prom ticket into a shimmery metallic clutch purse that resembled a bronze clamshell. She pulled down the passenger seat visor to check her makeup in the lighted mirror.

"You look a lot better than okay," Jordan replied truthfully. "You look spectacular."

"Thanks," Nisha said, flicking up the visor. She turned to Jordan. "And thanks again for coming back for me. You're a real friend," she said.

A real friend. Jordan nodded, unable to utter a response. Her body trembled, suddenly overcome with emotion as she thought of Tara. "This is so not how I pictured our prom turning out — or our friendships," she said finally. "I'm just glad that you don't hate me like Tara does."

"No way," Nisha replied, touching Jordan's arm. "I could *never* hate you. How could you even think that? And I'm sure that Tara doesn't hate you either."

So Tara kept Nisha in the dark about the truth, too. "She does," Jordan told her. "She admitted it that day in the food court. And believe me, she meant it." Jordan could still hear the words. *I hate you . . . I've always hated you. . . .* It hurt to even think about them.

"Oh," Nisha said, then fell silent.

Now I'm making things weird for Nisha, Jordan said to herself. *Exactly what I didn't want to do.* "Hey. Let's not talk about this anymore," she said. "Are you ready for the prom?"

Nisha fidgeted with her bracelet. "Ooh. I'm really nervous. I hope I don't hurl all over your car before we get there."

Jordan laughed, the tension broken. "Me, too," she said and stepped on the gas. They made it all the way to the Fairmont Hotel free and clear.

"What are you doing?" Nisha asked when Jordan bypassed the parking lot and pulled into the circular driveway.

"I'm dropping you off," Jordan said.

Nisha looked as if she were about to have a panic attack. "No, you have to come *in* with me, Jord."

Jordan glanced down at her scruffy jeans and black flats. "Nisha, I can't. I'm not dressed right. I don't even have a ticket."

Nisha clasped onto her arm. "Please, Jord. You *have* to," she begged. "I can't go in there by myself."

"Ow! Why are you freaking out so much?" Jordan asked, loosening Nisha's grip. She really didn't want to go in there.

"Because I'm grounded, for one, and I'm

at the prom," Nisha replied. "And Brian doesn't know I'm coming. And when I find him I'm going to tell him . . ." She lowered her voice to a whisper. ". . . that I *love* him. Remember?"

"Oh, riiiiight," Jordan said, but of course she knew all that. Dropping Nisha off outside of the prom was one thing, but going *in*? Her stomach soured at the thought of it. *If I go inside, not only will I feel stupidly underdressed, there's no doubt that I'd see Tara . . . and Nate. It'd be so awkward and weird. Which was the main reason I didn't want to go in the first place.* She looked at Nisha, who now had her hands clasped together and an imploring expression on her face. *I have to do it anyway,* Jordan thought. *Nisha needs my support.* She swung the car back around to the parking lot.

A few minutes later, Jordan tried to ignore her uneasiness — and the odd glances she received from the couples chatting on the grand terrace — as they climbed the marble stairs to the main entrance of the hotel. She hoped that the shy boy from the prom committee, Stuart, would be on ticket duty. She could probably get by him without a ticket. Or she'd even settle for Tara, who *had* to be understanding about Nisha, right? But when they arrived outside the ballroom, they found Jenny Brigger in her purple halter dress collecting tickets by the door.

"Nice of you to go all out for the prom," Jenny said, eyeing Jordan's jeans.

"Look, I paid for the prom last week, but I forgot my ticket at home," Jordan explained. "I'll only be a few minutes and then I'm leaving." She gestured to her outfit. "Obviously."

She was expecting one of Jenny's infamous protests, but instead the girl smiled, extended both her arms toward the door, and said, "Go right ahead."

Jordan squinted at her. "Really?" There had to be a catch.

Jenny nodded. "Please, be my guest," she said. "And when you see your *ex*-friend,

Tara? Tell her that I *didn't* forget about the Snow White display she trashed."

Snow White? Jordan didn't want to know. When she passed Jenny, she thought she heard the girl snicker and say, "This is gonna be good" underneath her breath. Jordan shot her a dirty look. *Does Jenny really think I came here to have a catfight with Tara? Sorry, but it's not going to happen. Even if I weren't here for the sole purpose of supporting Nisha I wouldn't embarrass myself like that. Seriously.*

Jordan was determined to go in and get out as quickly as possible, but her ideas faded when she and Nisha entered the ballroom. "Wow," Jordan breathed, admiring the decor. The place looked like a beautiful graduation gift, wrapped in flowing silver and blue tulle. "This is incredible."

The lights were dimmed and a disco ball was spinning overhead. The band was rocking out. Eyeing a few of the other seniors from the cheerleading squad going crazy on the crowded dance floor, Jordan smiled, almost wanting to join them, but it seemed as though they were having a fantastic time without her.

"Where's Brian?" Nisha wanted to know. "Do you see him, Jord?"

"Not yet," Jordan replied, scanning the rest of the room, but she did spot her photography teacher, Mr. Davis, and his balding ponytail. He was bopping his head and sipping a glass of punch as he strolled around with an older woman with short salt-and-pepper hair. *Good choice for a chaperone,* she thought, since the ex-hippie was pretty laid back.

A few minutes later, the band switched to a dreamy slow song. The crowd on the dance floor fanned out and Jordan heard Nisha gasp.

"Find him?" Jordan asked, following her friend's gaze. She expected to see Brian but instead was led to the couple near the band—to where Nate and Tara were dancing to a romantic song without an inch between them.

Jordan clenched her hands as she watched them sway easily to the music with their eyes closed. She had to admit that Tara looked stunning in a shimmering pink strapless gown, her hair shining and perfectly twisted into an elegant up-do. But Jordan was unable to decipher which hurt more: an ex-boyfriend finding a replacement so quickly or a best friend jumping in without a care.

The best friend part, Jordan determined. Even after their argument at the mall, in the back of her mind she was still hoping that it wasn't true, that Tara really hadn't set her sights on Nate. *But it* is *true*, she said to herself. *Look at them. There's no denying it.*

"Well, I guess Tara finally got what she wanted," Jordan muttered.

"Not quite," Nisha said.

Jordan was taken aback. What did she mean by *that?*

CHAPTER *Thirteen*

**How to Administer the Rhythmic Snap Test
(aka the Can-he-dance-or-does-he-just-THINK-
he-can Test)**

1) Play music with beat of choice (fast, slow,
   mixed).*
2) Say, "Hey, that is one fine beat! Don'cha think?"
   (or words of similar ilk).
3) Subject should respond positively. If not, pick
   different song.
4) Proceed to snap/toe tap/bob head in time (if
   possible).
5) Invite subject to join along.

6) *Not a dancer (N.A.D.) indicators include: lack of participation; sudden shyness; inability to snap, tap, or bob adequately; severe sweating after minimal exertion, etc.* **

Most boys are rhythmically challenged. Best to keep it simple.

**Proceed to dance floor with caution.*

Tara closed her eyes, trying to *feel* the moment as she swayed cheek-to-cheek with Nate on the dance floor. All the ingredients for romance were there: *Sultry music — check. Wistful ambiance — check. Dreamy date, who happened to be an excellent dancer — double check.*

So why wasn't Tara feeling it?

Nate nuzzled closer and she inhaled his fresh soapy scent, which had a slight undertone of spicy cologne. He smelled delicious, but . . .

Nothing, Tara thought. *What's my problem? It's Prom. Why can't I just enjoy the here-and-now?* She opened her eyes, knowing exactly why. *It's because I can't stop wishing*

170

that Nate was Victor — the boy I'm supposed *to be dancing with.*

And I can't help missing my friends. And Tara couldn't fake liking Nate more than she did, no matter how much she wanted to. Maybe she'd fantasized about dating him in the past, but when push came to shove, it was Victor who she really wanted to get close to on the dance floor.

Nate pulled away a bit and gazed meaningfully into her eyes. "Tara," he breathed, before pursing his lips slightly and leaning in . . .

Uh-oh, Tara thought, recognizing the approach. She turned her head just in time to give him the cheek, and he planted his lips there. "*Nate.* I already told you. I like Victor," she said in a warning tone.

I wonder if I should call Victor's cell phone after this song is over, she thought as she continued to dance. *It's been a few days. Maybe he's had time to cool off — enough to hear me out. I could ask him to meet me at a diner or something,* she mused. *Victor seeing me in this dress has got to improve my chance at forgiveness.*

"Come on, Tara. You can kiss me *once*, can't you?" he asked. "Please?"

Wow. Is he seriously begging? Tara thought. If Nate weren't the fantasy date of almost every girl at Emerson High, she'd say that he was dangerously bordering on pathetic. *What a major turnoff. Was he like this with Jordan?* She gave him a stern look. "How many times do I have to *tell* you?"

"It's just that now's the perfect time," he said. "I'd love to see Jordan's reaction. Wouldn't you?"

"Jordan's *here*?" Tara asked, her pulse quickening as she spun around. She couldn't be. Nisha had said Jordan was going to some music festival in Springfield with Emo Boy. Tara craned her neck to quickly scan the other couples on the dance floor, then the crowd around the room. "I don't see her," she said, turning back to Nate.

Who was leaning in to kiss her — *again!*

"Nate! What's the matter with you?" she asked, then realized that his lips were pointed in her direction, but his eyes were peeking over her shoulder. Then, when Tara turned to follow his line of vision, she saw her.

Even with her blond hair in a loose ponytail and wearing a pair of old jeans and a T-shirt, Jordan looked more beautiful than half the girls who'd spent hours getting ready for the prom. *Including me?* she wondered.

"Oh, I get it," Tara murmured, finally understanding what this was all about. "You don't really like me. You just want to date me to make Jordan jealous, *don't* you?"

Nate rolled his eyes and shrugged. "As if you don't want to get back at her, too," he said wryly.

Do I? Tara wondered. She had to think about it for a minute. Make that a second. "No. I don't," she said. "Not like this. As a matter of fact, I really miss Jordan."

And now that they weren't friends anymore, Tara was starting to believe that maybe this whole thing was more *her* fault than Jordan's. *Maybe if I'd spent less time worrying about Nate's feelings and more time being a best friend to Jordan, this wouldn't have gotten so out of hand.*

"Look, what's the big deal?" Nate said. "Just kiss me once. You *know* you *want* to," he said, pulling in closer.

Ew. "Excuse me while I go find a bucket to vomit in," Tara said, pushing away, but Nate didn't let her go.

"Tara . . ."

"Hey, Lombardo. I don't think the girl wants to dance with you anymore," Tara heard a boy declare from behind her. *Was it . . . ?* She spun around to see Victor in a wide stance, wearing the tux she'd picked out for him. His brown hair was short and tousled on the top like Nate's, his hazel eyes blazing.

"Victor! You're here!" Thrilled, Tara tried to go to him, but Nate was still holding her hand.

He narrowed his eyes at Victor. "Maybe

you should mind your own business, Kaminski."

"Tara *is* my business," Victor replied with matching venom. "She's my girlfriend."

"I am?" Tara asked, her face breaking into a joyous smile, which faded almost instantly as she glanced from one boy to the other. She didn't like where this was headed. She twisted her hand out of Nate's grip and the boys began to circle slowly, staring each other down. Tara knew that Nate could handle his own — he was a varsity athlete — but Victor?

She bit her bottom lip and glanced around. A crowd was beginning to form. Why wasn't anyone doing something to stop this? Where were the chaperones when you needed them?

"Guys, come on. This is silly," she began, but the boys weren't listening. She called for Mr. Davis.

"If she's your *girlfriend,* then why is she at the prom with *me?*" Nate asked with a smirk.

Victor roared. With fists up he charged at Nate, but Nate delivered a quick jab toward Victor's stomach. Victor blocked it. He swung at Nate's face . . . and missed.

Then Nate whacked him square in the nose.

Tara winced when she saw Victor's head flip to the side with the impact. He staggered back and fell to the floor, blood dripping from his nostrils.

"Victor!" Tara cried, rushing to him. "You idiot! He's bleeding!" she yelled at Nate.

Nate stood there with his mouth open. "Man, I'm sorry. I didn't think —"

Someone handed Tara a silver napkin from a table and she touched it to Victor's nose as she and a few others helped him up. By the time Mr. Davis arrived, it was all over.

"I'm fine," Victor told him. "I slipped and fell. No problem."

"Are you sure about that?" Mr. Davis asked, clearly not believing him. "Because if there happened to have been a fight, I could have the instigator thrown out of the party."

"I fell, Mr. Davis," Victor repeated.

"Okay." Mr. Davis nodded. "I'll let you boys work it out on your own for now but if there's another scuffle, you're *both* out."

Tara was about to tell Mr. Davis that there *had* been a fight and, technically, Nate had thrown the first punch. So maybe he should be the one to leave, right now. She stopped herself when she noticed that Victor was walking away!

"Victor. Wait," Tara said, following him across the ballroom. "Where are you going?"

"Home," Victor said, but he stopped when Tara touched his arm. "Ugh! I can't believe I got into it with Nate. I mean, I didn't want to give you up without a fight but it wasn't supposed to go like this." He removed the napkin and inspected his nose, which by now had stopped bleeding. "I thought I could win you over with my witty intellect. Now you must think I'm a stupid wimp." He turned to leave.

"But I don't, Victor! Don't go. You should rest. You might have a concussion or something," Tara said, wanting to cringe as the last few words poured from her mouth. What she'd meant to say was, *You should take me in your arms and kiss me because nobody has ever cared enough to want to fight for me — figuratively or physically. And I've never liked anybody as much as I like you, Victor.* But she couldn't get it out.

"I don't have a concussion," Victor told her. At least he wasn't running off anymore.

"You might. How do you know?" Tara asked, buying time until she gathered the nerve to tell him how she really felt. "Okay, let's just say for argument's sake that you *don't* have a concussion. Then why —"

It was then that Victor leaned in and kissed her, just as quickly as he had the night of their first date, only this time they managed to meet at the lips.

Before Tara had a chance to react, he kissed her again, a slower, more deliberate kiss that sent her body into shivers. She wrapped her arms around him and closed her eyes, feeling her head swirl.

"Wow, I — I . . ." Tara stuttered when they parted. "I really like you," she finally spat out. It wasn't eloquent, but at least it was better than saying he had a concussion.

"Me, too," Victor said. "I mean, *you*. Not me. I like *you*, too. Oh, God." He blushed. "Why can't I stop making a fool out of myself tonight?"

"Maybe we should shut up and dance," Tara suggested.

"Good idea." Victor took Tara's hand, but instead of showing her to the dance floor, he led her through a pair of French doors and onto a private terrace, barely lit by the light of the moon.

Tara could hear only a faint whisper of a

song from outside, but she didn't care as Victor twirled her around and then drew her near. "Did I tell you how beautiful you look tonight, T-Bone?" he asked her.

"No," Tara replied, looking up at him with a smile.

Victor grinned boyishly and replied, "Oh. Okay. I was just wondering."

"No fair!" Tara laughed and swatted him playfully, then looped her arms lightly around his neck to dance. And when she nestled her head on Victor's chest, he *did* tell her she was beautiful — inside and out — as they rocked and swayed underneath the starry sky.

CHAPTER *Fourteen*

"I — I can't believe that just happened," Nisha heard Jordan murmur as the excitement on the dance floor was breaking up.

"Where did Tara and Victor go?" Nisha asked. The band launched into an upbeat tune as couples began to dance again. "Do you think Victor is all right?"

"I think so," Jordan said, "and something tells me they probably want to be alone right now."

Nisha nodded. She'd like to be alone with Brian right now, too. If only she could find him.

"I guess I should go talk to Nate at some point," Jordan said. "See if he's okay." She paused. "Oh, look! There's your boyfriend," Jordan said, pointing across to the other side of the dance floor.

Nisha half-expected to see some nasty-looking guy with a toupee or someone who'd never in a million years be her boyfriend, since pointing out those kinds of guys was a running joke among her friends. She couldn't see past the kids dancing at first, but when she did, Brian was indeed there, sitting at an empty table playing with his cell phone. He looked forlorn but adorable in his tuxedo.

An instant later, Nisha's phone chirped inside her purse. She snapped open her clamshell to find that Brian had sent her a text.

☹ Miss u. What r u doing? ☹

Nisha's heart swelled as she quickly typed back.

Waiting 4 u 2 ask me 2 dance. Look up.

She pressed SEND and waited anxiously for Brian to get the message. A few seconds later, Brian was scanning the room. Nisha caught his eye and smiled.

Jordan murmured something about finding Nate and made a quick departure as Brian pushed his way through the dancers. When he reached Nisha, he swooped her into his arms and whirled her around. Nisha giggled and kicked her legs back as she hugged him tightly.

"How . . . ?" he asked, beaming with amazement when he'd set her back on her feet.

"I snuck out," Nisha admitted, for the first time feeling a wave of excitement about it. "I know I'm going to pay for it later, but I couldn't miss our prom." And now that she was there she intended to enjoy every minute of it. "So are you going to ask me to dance, or what?"

"Just a sec. I'll be right back," Brian said, motioning for her to stay put.

Nisha waited anxiously as she watched Brian whisper something to the bandleader, then jog back to where Nisha was standing. She gave him a questioning glance, but Brian just grinned and led her to the center of the dance floor.

A moment later the band transitioned into a cover of an old song by Madonna called "Crazy for You." Nisha smiled and stepped into Brian's open arms. "You remembered!" she said. "This song was playing during our first slow dance together. On our first date at the Coral Café!"

Nisha knew that she was a hopeless romantic, able to recall every detail of the evening, but she didn't realize that Brian was, too.

"First dance, first date . . . I wanted this song to be playing for something else, too," he said, holding her tightly as they circled the dance floor slowly.

"First prom?" Nisha asked.

Brian didn't answer right away. Instead they danced. He hugged Nisha as if he never wanted to let her go, and she didn't want him to. Then Brian tilted his head so that he could whisper into her ear. "I love you."

Nisha's heart danced in her chest. That was what he had meant. She wanted to tell him she loved him back right then. "I — I . . ." she began, but she couldn't bring herself to say the words.

Brian pulled away a bit. "It's okay. You don't have to say it if you're not feeling it, too," he said, though his face was clearly disappointed.

"No, it's not that," Nisha tried to explain. "It's just —" How could she tell him that she loved him when she was still lying to him about her family? She couldn't, not until she came clean. And she had to do it now before she lost her nerve. "I have to tell you something, Brian. And you're not going to like it."

"What is it?" Brian asked, suddenly looking very concerned.

Nisha led him by the hand off the dance floor and to an out-of-the-way table. And as the song was ending, she was finally, for the first time, truly and completely honest with Brian — about everything.

She explained how she never told her parents about him, and how her guru had. How her parents had grounded her and forbade her to attend the prom.

"So it wasn't all about a disrespectful tone of voice. It was about lying . . . and you," she said, finishing.

"And when your sister said that you talked about me all the time at home . . . ?" he asked.

"A lie." Nisha reached out to touch his hand, her throat tight. "She was trying to help me."

"Of *course* she was," Brian muttered. "How could I have been so brainless? Nisha, your parents must think I'm a total jerk for going along with all this." He shook his head and pulled his hand away.

He's right. They do, Nisha thought. "I mentioned that you wanted to meet them," she offered, "but I don't know if they heard me. They were pretty angry at the time." She searched Brian's eyes, which now seemed unsure, wary. "I'm sorry, Brian," she said, resisting the urge to defend her falsehoods. *No more excuses.* "I'm through with the lying. I promise." She hoped he could he forgive her.

Brian glanced back at the dance floor. "Where have I heard that one before?"

"Seriously," Nisha said. "You don't believe me?"

"How do I know you're telling me the whole truth?" Brian asked her. "How do I know that tomorrow you won't change your mind and forget what you're promising?"

"You have a point," Nisha agreed. There was only one way she could prove to Brian that she meant what she said. "You want to go meet my parents?"

Brian's jaw dropped. "You mean like, now? Leave the prom?" he asked as tiny beads of sweat appeared above his upper lip.

"I do," Nisha replied and stood. "Let's go find Tara and Jordan and tell them we're leaving."

"Uh, okay," Brian said, seeming a shade paler. He was clearly very nervous about what lay ahead.

So was Nisha. This time, though, she couldn't back away from the truth.

"There they are," Brian said, pointing to the table with the castle-like ice sculpture on it, which was melting fast.

"You mean they're *together*?" Nisha asked, swiveling her head in that direction. Brian was right. It seemed that her best friends were actually having a civil discussion over a plate of fruit near the punch bowl.

"You think they're making up?" Brian asked.

"I don't know. But sharing food is definitely a good sign," Nisha said, hanging back a little to give them some space. From her vantage point she could see Jenny Brigger in her purple dress making a beeline for Tara. "Ugh! Why does she have to butt into their conversation now?"

"This can't be good," Brian mentioned, quickening his pace. "Maybe we should head over."

Nisha agreed. By the time they got close enough, all she could make out were the words, *Snow, dwarfs,* and *who do you think you are?* coming from Jenny's mouth. However, it was what Nisha saw that was more important.

Jordan was munching on grapes by the edge of the table. Tara was next to her and motioning emphatically to Jenny, clearly trying to reason with the girl. Jenny, on the other hand, was frowning at Tara while clutching a glass brimming with frothy cherry punch.

I'll bet that witch is going to chuck it at Tara! Nisha realized and broke into a sprint. "Tara! Tara! Watch out!" she called, waving her hands.

Tara and Jordan looked over their shoulders to see who was shouting the warning. At the same time Jenny lifted her hand and released the liquid.

Jordan noticed what was happening and pulled Tara away. But it was too late for Nisha. All she could do was watch in horror as the sticky red fluid arced past her best friends and landed smack in the center of her own dress.

"Ahhhhhhhhh!"

Stunned and dripping, Nisha thought she heard a scream, but it wasn't her own. Apparently Tara and Jordan had doused Jenny with two cups of the same fate.

"I can't stress about this now," Nisha told Brian as she used a silver napkin to blot the enormous red stain on her dress, unsuccessfully, for the last time. "I have more important things to focus on."

That was for sure. Like how her parents were going to react when they a) found out that she had snuck out of the house to meet the boyfriend she wasn't supposed to be dating at the prom she wasn't supposed to be attending and they b) met said boyfriend.

I hope it doesn't get too ugly, Nisha thought. The odds were on her side, though. She and Brian were now in the limousine that Brian had rented for the prom, on their way to the Dixits' house, where Nisha's mother and father were having a relaxing visit. *My parents wouldn't completely freak in front of Mr. and Mrs. Dixit, would they?*

Nisha heard Brian draw in a sharp breath when the driver told them that they had arrived. She squeezed his hand. "Don't worry, it's all good," she reassured him, then stopped. *No more lying, remember.* "No, I take that back. It might be painful." She swallowed hard and followed him out of the limo and to the front door. She rang the bell.

Raj answered the door. "Hey," he said, looking from Nisha to Brian. He seemed surprised and deeply confused. "Um, what's up? You know your parents are here, right?"

"I know. We have to talk to them," Nisha explained. "They need to meet my boyfriend."

"Oh," Raj said, raking a hand through his thick wavy hair. "Um, good luck with that." He stepped back and opened the door wider, then led them through the kitchen to the patio out back. Nisha's parents and the Dixits were out there, enjoying the weather and some refreshing mango *lassies.*

"Beta!" Nisha's mother rose from her seat as soon as she saw her. "What happened to you? Are you all right? Why are you in your prom dress?" When Brian entered the backyard in his tuxedo, her eyes widened. "Is this that Brian boy?"

"Shovana, please," Nisha's dad said, touching his wife's arm. Then he faced his daughter. "What is it, Nisha? Why did you bring this boy here?"

The Dixits appeared speechless.

"I, um . . ." Nisha exchanged a glance with Brian. "I wanted you all to meet him," she said, placing her hands on Brian's arm.

Brian stepped forward to Nisha's father. "It's nice to finally make your acquaintance, sir," he said, shaking his hand. "I've heard a lot of great things about you." He then turned to Nisha's mother. "And I hear that you're an expert chef," he said with a smile, but Mrs. Khubani looked away. Then he greeted Mr. and Mrs. Dixit, and nodded to Raj. His jaw was clenched the whole time, but Nisha admired how brave he was being.

Brian was met with silence.

The tension was so thick, Nisha wasn't sure how to put what she had to say next. *Just say it,* she thought. "Mom, Dad. Brian is my boyfriend. We've been dating for a little more than six months."

"You've had a secret boyfriend for six months!" Mrs. Khubani cried.

Mrs. Dixit looked as if she were about to faint. "Nisha, how can you disgrace your family in our home?" she said. "Oh, Shovana, how sorry I feel for you — so, so sorry that you have such a disrespectful daughter who dates strangers off the street, no less!"

"He's hardly a stranger," Nisha said. "We've been going to the same school together for *four years*." Not that it was any of Mrs. Dixit's business. Then Nisha noticed the woman staring at her red-splotched dress. "Don't worry, it's a stain, not a fashion statement," she added.

Nisha glanced at Raj, who was squirming in the corner by a rose bush. Now would be a perfect opportunity for him to come clean about *his* secret *girl*friend, but it looked as if he were too busy wishing he were invisible. *Whatever. That's his choice,* Nisha thought.

Then she addressed her furious-looking parents. "You know, I snuck out of the house to surprise Brian at the prom tonight. I *could* have snuck back in and you guys would have never known the difference, but I didn't want to do that. I didn't want to lie to you. I can't live that way anymore. I want you to know me. The *real* me. So you can understand."

"Understand?" her mother said. "We already understand you. We're your parents."

"I know you try to," Nisha said. "But you couldn't possibly." She crossed over to the table where her parents were and sat in an empty seat across from them. "I am a girl who was born in India, but who understands English *way* better than she does Hindi. Who loves dancing *Kathak and* hip-hop. I love to eat homemade *gobi aloo* and frozen pizzas, too. Most of all, I'm a girl whose family means the world to her. But I also have a boyfriend who I care about, and who cares about me, and I'd really like you to get to know him one day."

She rose from her seat, and took Brian's hand. "But right now we have a prom to attend, and a ton of slow dances to dance. It's our last celebration as high school seniors and we can't miss another minute of it."

It was weird enough spending part of her prom at the Dixits' house and her parents seemed pretty stunned, so Nisha thought it was a good time to head for the door.

"Nisha, we cannot let you go to the prom after all of this," Mrs. Khubani piped up. "Lying and breaking your punishment and . . . this boy?"

Suddenly, Nisha's father tapped her mother's hand. "Shovana, let her go," Mr. Khubani said. "We can deal with it later. It took a lot of courage for our daughter to tell us these things. And this Brian fellow seems like a respectable young man."

Mrs. Khubani shook her head. "I don't like this one bit," she objected.

"I know it's not how we want it," Mr. Khubani said gently. "But in a few months our girl will be leaving us for college. If we don't let her go to the prom this dark cloud will hang over our family for the rest of the summer. We can discuss the issue just as well tomorrow, can't we?"

Nisha's mother sighed, then conceded with a slight nod.

Nisha ran back to kiss her father on the cheek. "Thanks, Dad."

"You're welcome," he said. "Now, *go* — before I change my mind."

"Okay." But first Nisha went over to her mother. "Thank you, Mom. Really," she said, and gave her a hug.

Her mom softened a little. "Don't be home late, *Beta*."

Nisha smiled and kissed her mom, too. "We're out," she said and headed back through the house and out the front door with Brian.

As soon as they were on the lawn, a wave of relief and elation washed over her. She was free from all the lies and pretending. She'd probably still have to face the consequences tomorrow, but at least Nisha knew she could finally be herself. *Hey, maybe this is what Kali meant by embracing it,* she thought.

"You were amazing back there," Brian said when they'd reached the limousine. He opened the car door for her and she slid onto the back seat. "Does this mean I get to learn more about the real you, too?" he asked, climbing in next to her.

"Everything," Nisha said. "The good, the bad, and the insane. But right now, I'm in the mood to dance!"

"To the prom!" Brian declared, pumping his fist cheesily as the driver started the car. "I just feel bad that you have to go back with your dress stained," he told Nisha. "We didn't even get any pictures."

Nisha glanced down at her ruined dress. "Not to worry," she said. "I have something else I can wear."

Twenty minutes later, Nisha was descending the steps of her home in the beautiful aquamarine sari and matching *choli* Kali had given her. Her sister was at the foot of the stairs, camera snapping, while Brian stood next to her with his tongue hanging out.

Okay, not really. But he did clearly like Nisha's outfit.

"You . . . you . . ." he sputtered.

"Look like a goddess?" Kali offered, and Brian nodded.

A few final photos in front of the limousine, and they were ready to go. "See you later, Kali! Don't wait up!" Nisha cried and waved as the car pulled away.

Nisha leaned back in the leather seat and exhaled. Brian swung his arm around her and Nisha nuzzled herself into the crooks of his body, finally able to relax.

"Too bad we can't have the band play our first song again," she said wistfully. "It's the first time I'm wearing a sari outside of the Indian community."

Brian kissed her on the top of her head, then began to hum the tune. "How's that?" he asked and continued humming.

"A little off key, but it'll work," Nisha teased him. Then she grew quiet because there was another first she had to do. "Brian? There's something I've been wanting to tell you for a long time," she said, pulling away so that she could gaze into his sweet blue eyes. She smiled shyly. "I . . . I love you, too."

"Really?" Brian stopped humming, then grew serious as he gently touched his lips to hers.

Nisha smiled into his kiss. It wasn't the first time Nisha had kissed her boyfriend. And she now knew it wouldn't be the last.

CHAPTER *Fifteen*

"Talk about an exciting prom," Jordan told Tara later that night as they sat at a table by the dance floor. "First a fist-fight —

"Correction. An *accident*," Tara said, with a serious look in her eyes. "I told you. Victor *fell*, remember?"

"Oh. Right. An *accident*," Jordan said, going with it. "Then the cherry punch incidents . . . I can't believe what a witch Jenny Brigger is. She totally ruined Nisha's dress."

"*I* can," Tara replied. "But at least we got back at Jenny. Dumping punch on her was the highlight of my senior year."

"I thought the prom was the highlight of your year — and *Victor*," Jordan said, teasing her a little. "You guys seem pretty cozy." She hoped she wasn't stepping over the line with the comment. Jordan was glad to be on speaking terms with Tara again, but it wasn't exactly comfortable and definitely not on a best friend level.

Tara blushed. "I think maybe we are — finally," she said. "I really like him. He's so funny and sweet."

"Not to mention cute," Jordan added, "thanks to your makeover."

"That too," Tara admitted, "but for some reason, it doesn't seem so important anymore."

Of course it didn't, Jordan thought, wishing she hadn't mentioned it because now there was an awkward break in the conversation. She turned to watch the kids on the dance floor, unsure if it was her cue to apologize to Tara for being so stubborn about hearing her out, which played a major part in ruining their friendship, or if it was her cue to leave. *Just do it, Jord. Apologize. You know you want to.*

"So, I, um . . . where is Victor now?" she asked, chickening out.

"He went to get something out of his car," Tara answered. "He should be right back."

"Oh."

Another lull.

Jordan glanced at Tara, who was nervously untying and retying the satin bow on her dress. *Maybe the prom isn't the right place to do this. Maybe Tara can't wait for me to get lost,* she thought. *But if I don't apologize now, I might never get the chance again.*

"Tara, I'm sorry!" she blurted out.

At the same time, Tara said, "Jordan, I miss you!"

"You do? Really?" Jordan asked, tears of joy stinging her eyes.

"So much." Tara was nodding and wiping away her own tears. A second later both girls were hugging each other.

"This is all my fault, Jordan," Tara said

when they had parted. "I should have been a better friend. I should have supported you. I was so stupid."

"No." Jordan grabbed Tara's hands. "I should have at least given you the benefit of the doubt," she replied. "I wouldn't even listen to you. And I said all those mean things about you wanting to get with Nate. No wonder you hated me."

"But I *don't*. I didn't mean it. You know that, right?" Tara asked. "I could never *ever* hate you. Okay?"

She searched Jordan's eyes so earnestly that Jordan believed her. "Okay," she said, relieved.

"But . . ." Tara continued, "if I'm going to be totally truthful here, you have to know something."

Uh-oh. Jordan had a bad feeling about this.

Tara took a deep breath and then said, "You were right about Nate. I did have a crush on him — before Victor."

"What?" Jordan pulled back. "You mean you *were* trying to hook up with him?"

"No!" Tara gasped. "God, no. I mean, I liked him, so that's why I was defending him so much when you started seeing Shane. But, I swear, that time you saw Nate and me together in the school courtyard I really was trying to mend *your* relationship with him. I felt so guilty for telling Nate about Shane that I wanted to fix things, but I only made them worse."

Jordan thought back to the day she saw Nate and Tara talking closely in the courtyard. She had been so blind with anger then, but now she could see how Tara's story made sense.

"And then when you wouldn't listen to me, I got mad," Tara went on. "And Nate and I started hanging out. I thought we were becoming friends but he was only using me to make you jealous. That's why he kissed me in front of you — and that's why he asked me to the prom."

Jordan shook her head. "I know I hurt him, but that was a pretty jerky thing for Nate to do — to you *and* to me."

"Tell me about it. It almost cost me my relationship with Victor," Tara said, just as her cell phone jingled like an old fashioned telephone.

"New ring tone?" Jordan asked.

Tara snapped open her evening bag and retrieved her phone. "I got sick of Beethoven's Ninth." She viewed the caller ID. "It's Victor. I'll only be a minute."

As Tara took the call, Jordan wondered if maybe it was time for her to go. Tara and Victor deserved some romantic time alone. After all, it *was* the prom.

"I'm going to head home," Jordan said, standing, when Tara had hung up.

"No, stay!" Tara leapt out of her seat. "You can't leave. We have so much more to talk about. Victor won't mind."

"Oh, I don't know about that." Jordan had a lot more she wanted to tell Tara, too, but it could wait. And as tempting as it was to hang out with them all night she couldn't exactly have fun at the prom in jeans and flats when everyone else was decked out. "We can talk more tomorrow."

Tara shrugged. "Oh, well. Go ahead. I guess that means you don't want your surprise . . ." Tara said breezily.

"Surprise?" Jordan repeated, breaking into a smile. She was always a sucker for surprises. "What is it?"

Tara beamed. "You'll see," she said, linking her arm with Jordan's, leading her away from the table. "It should be waiting for us in the powder room."

"I know. It's a roll of toilet paper!" Jordan joked.

Tara laughed. "Close, but no."

It was then that Jordan spotted him and froze. Leaning on a tulle-covered wall, Nate was huddled with Moose and Sam from the baseball team. She'd tried, unsuccessfully, to find him after the incident with Victor and had assumed that he'd left the party. "I should probably take care of this," she said, gesturing slightly in Nate's direction.

Tara nodded. "Good luck," she said. "I'll meet you in the ladies' room."

Jordan's stomach flipped nervously as she crossed over to him. What was she supposed to say? Earlier she'd wanted to ask Nate what the fight with Victor was all about, but now Jordan wanted to rail on him for using her best friend to get back at her. But they were at the prom. Maybe they should just try to make amends.

Sam was the first one to see her and he tapped Nate on the shoulder. A moment later, Nate's soft brown eyes were locked onto her.

"Hey, Jordan. Nice dress," he said with a snort.

Jordan glanced down at her jeans. *So, it's going to be like that,* she thought with a sigh. "Can I talk to you for a minute?"

"About what?" Nate asked.

Jordan rolled her eyes. "Just come on," she said, pulling him away.

"She totally wants to get back with me," he said to his friends as they left.

When they were far enough away, Jordan dropped his arm. "Look. I'm really sorry about how everything turned out," she said. "But there's no reason for you to keep acting this way."

"Acting what way?" Nate asked, playing dumb.

"Like a jerk," Jordan said plainly.

"A jerk?" he repeated. "I'd say you were the jerk. You're the one who dumped me weeks before the prom. You humiliated me in front of the whole school."

"Nate, it's not like I planned to hurt you," Jordan said. "I'm sorry that it happened the way it did, but you didn't have to bring Tara into all this."

"Are you kidding me?" Nate asked, raising his voice. "If it wasn't for *you*, I would have never come here with Tara. And I would have never punched out Victor. As far as I'm concerned this whole thing is your fault. Do you even know how totally humiliated I was tonight?"

That makes two times he mentioned that. It was as if something clicked inside Jordan's brain. Nate wasn't upset over losing her as much as he was about being dumped.

"I'll admit the way we broke up was totally wrong," Jordan told him. "That's all on me. But I'm not the one who embarrassed you tonight, Nate. You did that all on your own." She started away but stopped with one more thing left to say. "You know, when we first broke up I felt so guilty. I kept hoping that we could be friends again one day. But now . . . not so much."

This time she walked away and never looked back.

"How can you have a surprise for me, Tara? You didn't know I was coming to the prom," Jordan said later in the pink powder room of the Fairmont Hotel. "*I* didn't even know I was coming."

Jordan was definitely glad she did, though. If she hadn't, she might never have bumped into Tara at the punch table, and they might never have bonded over slamming Jenny Brigger, and they definitely would never have apologized to each other, starting them on the road back to friendship.

"It wasn't exactly planned," Tara admitted, "so let's just call it fate, okay?"

Jordan heard a light rapping on the door. "Tara?" Victor's voice sounded from the other side.

"Just a sec," Tara said, gliding across the rug and out of the room. A moment later, she returned, carrying in a one-shouldered white silk gown on a hanger. A pair of strappy rhinestone sandals identical to her own dangled from her fingertips. She offered them to Jordan.

Jordan gasped, accepting the garments. "My prom gown?" she asked, astonished. "How?"

Tara shrugged and smiled. "The day after

I saw your gown in the consignment shop, Victor and I went back to buy it. I was still mad at you, but I couldn't see anyone else wearing the dress. It was made for you, Jord!" She gestured to the shoes. "Those I bought for myself on the same day, but I left them in Victor's trunk. Then when we broke up I felt too weird asking for them so I just bought myself another pair." She kicked up her foot, displaying a sparkly sandal. "Aren't you glad I did?"

"Tara, *you're unbelievable!*" Jordan declared. *"Thank you!"* She quickly removed her jeans and tee and slipped into the silky gown and the luxurious heels. Then she gave her friend a huge squeeze. "You're such a good friend — even when we were fighting you were thinking of me!"

Tara pulled away, her face turning solemn. "I'm not, Jord. I'm not a good friend at all. Sometimes I . . . I get so *jealous* I can't see straight," she admitted. "You're so beautiful and creative and people just seem to fall in love with you wherever you go. You don't even have to *try*."

She's jealous of me? "Are you crazy?" Jordan asked. "Look at yourself." She pointed Tara toward the mirror. "You're totally *gorgeous*. Not only that, you can do anything you set your mind to. No matter how impossible it might seem, you *always* make it happen. You're totally together, like, *all the time*. Sometimes I wish I were more like *you*," she confessed.

"Seriously?" Tara seemed surprised. "You don't think I'm obsessed with achievement?"

"Well . . ." Jordan pretended to consider the question. "Maybe a little, but that's what makes you so lovable."

Tara rolled her eyes and laughed. Then she pulled Jordan into an enormous hug.

"What?" Jordan asked innocently. "You have a really sweet boyfriend who seems to think so, too, right?"

"I do, don't I?" Tara said.

And when they parted Jordan could see that her friend was beaming, which made her do the same.

"I hear Shane's a great guy, too," Tara added, right before she swore she'd never utter the words *Emo Boy* or *Nail Polish Guy* again. "So. When do I get to meet him?"

"Soon," Jordan replied, suddenly wishing that Shane were with her at the prom. *He and his friends must have reached Springfield by now. Probably toasting marshmallows by the campfire and chatting about the bands they're dying to see at the Punktopia festival.* She pushed the thought away. "Are we ready to go out there?" she asked Tara.

"Not yet." Tara pulled the ponytail holder out of Jordan's hair and used it to twist the tresses into an elegant chignon just above the nape of Jordan's neck. A little powder, blush, and lip gloss . . . "*Now* we're ready," she declared.

Jordan and Tara exited the ladies' room, and the band was still rocking when they stepped into the party. As soon as they reached their table, they were greeted by Victor, Brian, and Nisha, who was no longer in her stained yellow gown but was wearing a beautiful aquamarine-colored sari!

"You look incredible!" Jordan and Tara cried at once.

"Thanks!" Grinning, Nisha's gaze went from Jordan to Tara. "So you guys are good?" she asked hopefully.

Jordan exchanged a glance with Tara and nodded. "I am. Are you?" she asked Tara.

"Totally."

"Great!" Then Nisha linked arms with her girls and whispered, "I told Brian the L-word," before shouting, "Let's party everybody!"

Jordan watched in awe as Nisha led the way to the dance floor. She wasn't sure if it was the beautiful sari or if it was because Nisha was in love, but her friend was simply luminous. Nisha raised her arms in the air, swung her hair and her hips, and danced as if nobody was watching. Brian, Tara, and Victor formed a circle around her. Jordan joined in, too, shaking it alongside her friends.

A few songs later the band wound down to a slow tune and Jordan felt a bit awkward as her friends paired off. She offered to watch the purses at the table, but Tara said, "Oh, no, you don't," and slung her arm around Jordan's shoulders. And they laughed and giggled, doing an embellished sway to the music.

Before they knew it, Principal Harris was clearing the dance floor to announce the prom queen and king. Jordan, Tara, Nisha, Victor, and Brian moved to the sidelines.

Jordan's heart pounded as she awaited the announcement, and Tara took her hand and squeezed it.

"For this year's prom queen, I give you . . ." the principal paused for dramatic effect.

Come on, Jordan thought. *Tara Macmillan. Say it. Say it!*

"Jorrrrdaaaaaan Taaaaaayllllllorrr!" he cried.

Huh? Jordan thought as the room erupted in applause.

She'd pulled out of the race, but the seniors had voted her in anyway? Jordan took a cautious glimpse at Tara, who was clapping just as wildly as the rest of the crowd.

"Looks like you can't get out of being Emerson's prom queen no matter how hard you try," she said with a genuine grin.

"I guess you're right," Jordan replied, laughing.

"Go and get your crown, girl!" Nisha cried.

Jordan smiled and stepped carefully onto the dance floor, waving at her friends and fellow students. When she reached Principal Harris she bent down so that he could place the sparkling crown atop her head.

She waved again at her classmates, thinking about how weird it was that high school was almost over. She was so different now than when she was a freshman. Actually, she'd changed a lot in the past few weeks, too.

But mostly she was thinking about how happy she was that she'd stayed at the prom — not because she won the title of prom queen, but because she was spending these final moments of high school with her friends, creating memories.

I just hope Nate doesn't spoil it by acting like a jerk during the royalty dance, she thought, since it was obvious that he was about to win. And a moment later the principal was announcing his name.

"Nate Lombaaaarrrrrddddddooooo!"

Jordan clapped along with the crowd, whose applause was just as enthusiastic for Nate as it had been for Jordan. She scanned the swarm of students in the ballroom, waiting for him to emerge with his arms raised overhead and hamming up the walk to get his crown.

But Nate didn't appear.

The principal called his name again, then twice more, and still no Nate.

Where is he? Jordan wondered, beginning

to feel uncomfortable standing there alone. *He didn't* leave, *did he?*

Apparently, he had.

"Well, er, this is highly unusual," Mr. Harris said, wiping a palm across his perspiring forehead. "The king and queen are supposed to dance together. Who's going to dance with Jordan?"

"I am."

Jordan's head whipped in the direction of the voice, just as Shane pushed forward through the crowd. He was wearing a black single-breasted pinstriped tuxedo jacket with matching close-cropped pants and black high-top sneakers. His black hair was spiked a bit on top, with a fringe still hiding his right eye.

Jordan gasped, speechless, as he strode toward her and took her in his arms. He stared at her with his dark, intense eyes. "Sorry I'm late."

She smiled at him, her heart feeling as if it were about to burst. "You came back for me," she murmured. She was unaware that the music had started and the principal had left them until Shane began to glide her around the dance floor. "I don't understand . . . ?"

"Caitlyn and Mark split up and I took the opportunity to ride back with Caitlyn and her sister," Shane explained. "I had a feeling you'd end up at the prom. And if you were going to be there, I wanted to be there with you. So . . ."

That was all Jordan need to hear. She reached up and kissed Shane on the lips. "Thank you." Then she rested her head on his shoulder as they danced.

Moments later, couples began to drift onto the dance floor alongside of them. Jordan noticed Victor and Tara dancing nearby, while Nisha and Brian were at the far end in a romantic embrace.

"Hey, want to meet the infamous Tara?" Jordan whispered to Shane. But before she had a chance to introduce him, Tara leaned in and said, "Jordan, is this the infamous Shane?"

And everyone laughed.

Soon the song shifted into a faster beat — a cover of an old tune called "We Are Family." Nisha came running over with Brian in tow. "Ooh! I *looooove* this song!" she cried, swiveling her hips. "It's like the girlfriend anthem!"

"Let's go!" Jordan said as she and Tara bopped with Nisha to the center of the dance floor. Shouting the lyrics at the top of their lungs, the girls barely noticed that the guys had hung back to let them do their thing.

When the song was almost over, Jordan linked arms with her friends, forming a tight circle.

"Guys, do you realize we finally made it to the prom? And we all look fabulous!" Nisha said. "Oh, and the boys aren't bad either."

"I can't believe our senior year is almost over already. I'll bet the summer flies by even faster," Tara said. "Good thing I'm almost finished packing for college."

Jordan looked at her. "You are *not* packed," she said then tilted her head. "Are you?"

"Just one small bag," Tara admitted and Nisha laughed.

So did Jordan, but inside she was feeling a little shaky. In a couple of short months she'd be off to Northwestern University. What if college was too hard? What if she got lonely? Jordan was just getting used to high school, maybe she wasn't ready to leave. She definitely wasn't ready to part with her friends.

"Hey, what's up?" Tara asked her. "Why so quiet?"

"It's just . . . I'm gonna miss you guys!" Jordan declared, feeling close to tears.

"So am I!" Tara said, nodding.

"Me, too!" Nisha exclaimed. The girls cried and clung to each other tightly as the song finally ended.

Moments later, the boys joined the circle

while the band played Shakira's "Hips Don't Lie."

"Can I cut in?" Victor asked, taking Tara's hand, and the two of them began to boogie.

Of course, Brian and Nisha did the same.

Moving to the music, Jordan glanced at Shane. "You ready for this? I know it's your favorite song," she said, even though she was sure the opposite was true.

"Are *you*?" He asked, grinning, then grooving to the beat surprisingly well. It wasn't long before the future's uncertainty melted away from Jordan's thoughts.

Because after all, it *was* the prom.

A time to celebrate — to savor the last moments of high school with your closest friends.

And Jordan, Tara, and Nisha spent the rest of the night, right there on the dance floor, doing just that.

Together.

EPILOGUE

"Come on, Jordan!" Tara called the next day, from the backseat of Jordan's SUV. "We've got to get on the road. We're already late."

Jordan skipped down the front steps of the school clutching the folder containing her photography project. She ran straight to her mom's SUV and opened the driver's side door and climbed in.

"Well?" Shane asked from the passenger seat.

"Yeah," Nisha leaned forward from Brian's lap in the back. "What did you get on your introspective?"

Jordan opened the folder to show them her grade. "An A!" she squealed. "Mr. Davis said it was the best piece he'd seen all year!"

"Hallelujah," Victor said, raising his hands in the air, followed by a swat from Tara, who was beside him.

"I guess this means we're ready for Punktopia?" Shane asked. "If we hurry we can make it in time to see the Rabid Poets' Society."

"The who?" Nisha asked.

"That's a classic rock band, babe," Brian said.

"Do *not* tell that joke again," Tara warned him.

"How about this one? To *Punktopia*!" he cried, raising his fist.

"NO!" Tara said.

Jordan laughed and started the car. "We may be ready for Punktopia, Shane, but is Punktopia ready for *us*? That's the *real* question."

As she pulled away from the high school, she listened to her friends tease each other. It was hard to believe that in a few short weeks they'd be graduating. Then in a few more weeks after that they'd be starting their first years of college.

It was so exciting. So full of possibilities. So scary.

Will we achieve all of our dreams? Will we discover new ones? What will we be like in the years to come, when high school feels like a distant memory?

Jordan still wasn't sure about any of it, but two things were certain. She'd always love Tara and Nisha, her best friends forever, and she'd never forget the night of their senior prom.

*Craving more romance from
Jeanine Le Ny?*

Check out

Turn the page for a sneak peek!

Two days later, the sky was blue and cloudless and the scent of sardines barely noticeable as Nikki pedaled her first deliveries toward the Pelican Island Bridge. Her phone rang to the tune of a spunky salsa beat and Nikki bobbed her head to a few bars as she checked out the screen. *Cool,* she thought, *a text from Blair.* She pulled to the side of the road to take a look.

helllllllp! Muffy strks again! what up w/u?

Nikki laughed, imaging how Blair's annoying cousin was torturing her friend. She keyed a quick message with her news:

Met hot boy.

She pressed SEND and her phone rang almost instantly. She glanced at the screen. Blair, of course.

"What's his name? What does he look like? When are you going out?" Blair babbled as soon as Nikki picked up.

"It's Daniel. He's really cute in that shaved-head-alterna-boy kind of way, and I don't even know if he likes me yet. I'm on a quest to find out . . . and to get his digits. I'll keep you posted."

"You'd better," Blair said. "And I hope you're wearing that cute white mini that shows off your legs. That'll get his attention."

"You think?" Nikki asked, glancing down at that very skirt. She didn't want to admit that yesterday and today she'd put on extra-hot outfits hoping to run into Daniel. Needless to say, her mom had been happy to see Nikki in a skirt again, but now that Nikki had it on she wasn't so sure it was a good idea. And maybe she should have left the kitten-heeled slides in the closet, too, even if they were fabulous. Oh, well.

"Ugh, here comes Muffy with her tennis racquet," Blair whispered.

Nikki heard a scuffling sound, then a soft thud. "Where are you?" she asked.

"Towel hut," Blair whispered. "I can't play another game of tennis, Nik. We just got here and she's already wiped the court with me six — oh, gotta go!" *Click*.

Nikki almost felt sorry for Blair, but not quite. *At least things are looking up on my end*, she thought, flipping her phone shut and hopping back on the bike to begin her deliveries. She was bound to run into Daniel again sooner or later.

By the time she'd reached the end of her twelfth run without a single Daniel sighting, however, Nikki had resigned herself to the fact that it was probably going to happen later rather than sooner. As she pedaled across the bridge back to Pelican Island her mind raced with thoughts about the cute boy with the intense eyes.

She wondered who he was. A tourist? She'd never seen him before but then that didn't mean anything. She didn't know every guy in Richfield and/or the surrounding area. But then again, if he did live around here he'd probably be vacationing on Bella Island with everybody else.

Nikki glided to a halt in front of the Italian Scallion and parked the bike against the building. *So if Daniel's a tourist, that means he'll be leaving by the end of the summer, at the latest,* she said to herself.

She shook her head. *What are you doing, Nikki? You don't even know if he likes you and you're already stressing about when he's leaving?* She decided to think about the way he said her name instead. *Nikki, Nikki, Nikki. . .*

"You wanna talk to *who*?" Nikki heard Dad saying into the telephone when she entered the shop. "My daughter? Why? Who's this?"

Nikki gasped. She knew exactly who it was! Or at least she *hoped* she knew. It made sense now. Daniel didn't ask for her home number because she'd already given him her *work* number — on the menu! Clever guy. "I'll take it. It's my friend," she told her father, who handed over the phone, then disappeared in the kitchen. "Hello?" she said into the receiver.

"Uhhhh, is this Colie?" a boy's gruff voice said over the line.

"Daniel?" she asked, though now that she'd heard him she wasn't so sure. At the same time she wondered, *How does he know about Colie? He knows me only as Nikki.*

"Yeah, that's me," the guy breathed. "Want to go out tonight? I hear you're an awesome kisser."

Girls giggled in the background. "Shhh!" someone said through the laughter.

Now she knew it wasn't Daniel. "Who is this?" she demanded.

"You know," the guy said through a snicker. "Danny."

The girls cackled louder right before Nikki slammed the phone into its cradle on the wall. "What jerks!" she muttered.

Paul walked by with a case of soda on his shoulder. "Who's a jerk?"

Couldn't she have a second of privacy? "Nobody," Nikki replied, though she had a feeling she knew who was behind the prank call. With no Caller ID on the store phone, she picked up the receiver again and dialed *69 to see if she could find out who was playing with her. She jotted down the recorded number and then dialed it.

"Bella Island Jitney!" a girl answered with a singsongy tone. "How may I help you?"

Nikki slammed the phone again. "Jerks!"

"Who?!" Paul asked again, this time from the drinks refrigerator.

"Nobody!" Nikki cried and stormed to the door of the shop. On the way out she heard Vince ask Paul, "What's her problem?"

Oh, Nikki had a problem, all right. Three of them: Hannah, Stephanie, and Margaret. And she knew how the game went down. She couldn't just let this prank go unchecked.